R H Carter
The Kimble Detective

GW01403365

Full Name: Roy Howard Carter
Hometown: Magnetic Island, Queensland, Australia

Born in the UK, R. H. Carter spent a few years with the R.A.F. before being medically discharged with a back injury. He then spent many years flying a desk in the corporate world (which was never really him), before turning to the world of online marketing. In that realm he is a successful coach, mentor and international public speaker and is the author of a number of non-fiction books such as, 'Can A Beer Mat Change Your Life?', which is a compilation of his popular monthly newsletter *'Letters From A Small Island'*.

Hankering after the Mediterranean lifestyle, he moved to Cyprus and spent ten happy years there with his wife Lyn, before moving to another (much smaller) island, this time in the Coral Sea, in Queensland, Australia. 'Maggie', as Magnetic Island is affectionately known, is the place he and Lyn now call home and it is here that Roy has settled down to enjoy writing fiction.

Reason For His Love of Writing Fiction: Roy first got the bug for writing fiction after his primary school teacher gave him an A+ for his essay *'Life Inside A Ping-Pong Ball''* when he was ten years old.

Favorite film: *The Shawshank Redemption*

Favorite food: Beef Rendang. A good juicy steak with corn on the cob. A bacon sandwich.

Favorite Tipple: A nice glass (ok then, a bottle) of Barolo. Red Breast 12 year old Whiskey.

Favorite place to visit: Any beautiful tropical island.

For More information about R. H. Carter: Visit his Author Blog at:-

www.RHCarter-author.com

Follow Roy on Facebook:

www.facebook.com/r.h.carter.author

CARS, CATS & CROOKS

The Kimble Detective Agency Series

(BOOK 1)

R H CARTER

Published by
R&L Book Creation

Cover design by www.anniemoril.com

COPYRIGHT

Cover design by www.anniemoril.com

Createspace ISBN: 978-1503120440

CHAPTER ONE

"**W**HO D'YOU THINK you are, bloody Sherlock Holmes?" Sherri was looking at him quite blankly with her hands on her hips and a slightly annoyed expression on her face. "This is some kind of mid-life crisis, isn't it?"

"No, no, not at all," Peyton insisted, a smile on his face. He was quite amused by how she was reacting to this but in all honesty, he'd expected something of the sort. He had to admit it probably sounded a little ridiculous when said aloud. "I've always wanted to be a detective."

"Since when?" his wife scoffed. "You've never mentioned it before."

"Because I never thought I could do it before. Plus, I never had the opportunity."

His new redundancy from the car factory had given him just the chance he'd been waiting for, the chance he'd been longing for his entire life, and Peyton Kimble was going to seize it with both hands. He'd always felt wasted and frustrated; the same dead end job nearly his entire life, the dull monotony of the nine to five, the pain of knowing that he could have been so much more if he'd actually got his head together and gone to university when he'd had the chance. At the time he'd been a bit of a waster, more interested in hanging out with his mates, getting drunk and trying to pull girls than studying, and he was quite convinced he'd brought shame upon the entire family, or at least disappointed them quite severely. Then there was the added annoyance of having to watch his brother Arthur do so well for himself, flying high in his career with the police force, getting all the excitement and adventure that Peyton craved. It wasn't that he was jealous of his brother's success – not at all – he was happy for him and the pair of them usually got on well. He just knew that he could do the job equally as well as Arthur could, and that fact compounded his frustration.

"Why don't you just apply for another job?" Sherri was continuing to drone on, although by now he was only half listening to her, already excitedly thinking about what he would call his detective agency and whether he should change his name to something a little more intriguing. Would he need an assistant? Surely every good detective should have an assistant. But whom? They would need to be clever and smart, able to keep up with intricate theories and details.

"You have a decent enough CV, I'm sure you'll be able to find something..."

Peyton came out of his daydream, slightly surprised to find Sherri was still trying to convince him not to do this.

"The job market's rubbish at the moment, love, you know that. I'm better off doing this."

"Doing what?" she laughed. "You don't even know what you're doing! You don't even know *how* to be a detective!"

"Yes, I do," he insisted, trying not to get annoyed.

"Oh what, because you've read some Agatha Christie? Get real, Peyton. It's not going to work."

"Yes, it is," he answered back quickly, raising his voice slightly for the first time as he grabbed his coat off the back of the chair and swiped his keys off the top of the breakfast bar.

"Where are you going?" she asked with a sigh, turning to the kettle as it finished boiling, finally.

"I need to find myself an office," he announced. "If you're not going to support me in this then there's no point me working from home. We'll just get on each other's nerves, love, and I don't want us to end up bickering."

And that was that.

That was the start of the Kimble Detective Agency.

It was never supposed to be a family affair, but when Peyton received a call from his sister Rosaline later that afternoon, he found her surprisingly excited about the new venture, and quite insistent that she get involved in some manner. He could tell she was working her way round to asking him something straight away. It was just that tone in her voice, the way she was being all chatty and friendly, asking him all sorts of questions and acting overly encouraging. It was just her style. He'd learnt it well over the many years he'd known her.

He was standing in the middle of his brand new office at the time, the phone pressed to his ear as he rotated round in a circle, taking everything in. He glanced up from the corners of the skirting boards to the small spotlights installed on the ceiling, then tried to figure out where the furniture would go. It was the fourth one he'd seen that day, since leaving the house, and in general, he liked it the most. It had the correct combination of size, value for money, potential and location. Less than two miles from their home but near enough to the centre of town to be able to attract more business, it was about the same size as their living room and would easily accommodate two desks, a mini kitchen area with a microwave, kettle and fridge, and a couple of filing cabinets. Maybe even a small two seater sofa in the corner where their clients could sit and discuss cases with them when they came in for their first consultation. It would be nice to make them feel relaxed, he thought to himself as he tried to balance the multi-tasking of speaking to his sister whilst making a decision on the property.

"Just...hold on one second," he said down the mouthpiece of his mobile phone, then pulled it away from his ear and clasped his hand over it whilst he spoke to the estate agent. "I like it. I'll take it."

"Excellent," the slick suited young man smiled. "I'll just put a call through to the office and we'll get the paperwork drawn up." He in turn took out his own flashy smartphone and left the room.

Peyton pressed the phone to his temple again. "Hey Ros..."

"Yeah, so as I was saying," she continued chatting away enthusiastically. "You definitely need an assistant."

"Well, every good detective does," he quickly quipped cheerfully, whilst at the same time warily wondering where she was going with this. He and Ros had always got on well, but he couldn't actually imagine her being his assistant.

"You should probably think about a change of image too," she added. "You don't look much like a detective in those ghastly jumpers you wear."

Peyton instinctively looked down at his woolly jumper defensively. It looked alright to him. "What? Why not?"

"Because...well...they're not exactly stylish, are they, Peyt? You look more like a Geography teacher."

"Huh, there's nothing wrong with teachers, I married one."

"Just...let me be your stylist or something," Rosaline continued with a chuckle. "And let Jack be your assistant."

There. He knew it had been coming. Or at least, he knew *something* had been coming.

Jack was her son. Jackson Chadwick was his full name. He'd just turned eighteen years old and was definitely what Peyton would call a drop out. He spent more time smoking weed and playing on his Xbox than studying, which was probably one of the main reasons why he'd failed his A-levels and been unable to get on his chosen career course, whatever it was. As far as Peyton was concerned, the lad didn't have any drive in life and would probably be unreliable. Besides which, he'd never particularly got on great with kids and he was fairly sure Jackson disliked him.

He and Ros had lived with them for nearly a year after she'd split from her husband. It had been one of those messy divorces; similar to the one their parents had had many years previously. He'd got to know the kid quite a bit during that time, but Peyton had never particularly been one for children anyway. Sherri had always wanted them, and he would have been more than happy to give them to her. They always said it was different with your own anyway, and he would have done anything to please her. Only problem was, Sherri couldn't have kids. They'd talked about adoption at one point. Sherri had been an orphan herself. She'd grown up in a children's home and eventually got taken on by a couple similar to them who couldn't have kids of their own. She knew what it was like, what it felt like, to be all alone and thinking you were unwanted. Although Peyton couldn't empathise, having never gone through the experience himself, he was sympathetic and supportive of their discussions about adoption. But then Ros and Jack had come along.

The divorce had been quite sudden and unexpected, or at least, as far as Peyton was concerned it was. He hadn't really heard from his sister for a couple of months and had no idea that the relationship wasn't going well. She'd ended up virtually out on the streets and with nowhere to live. His brother Arthur already had a full house with a kid of his own anyway, and Sherri seized on the opportunity before he'd even had a chance to say no. Not that Peyton would have said no. He was a decent enough bloke. He wouldn't have turned away his sister and her kid in their hour of need. And so, they stayed.

Jack and Peyton hadn't exactly got on very well from the offset. He'd always had the impression Jack didn't like him, and he'd found the kid to be obnoxious and cocky, purposely flouting his rules and causing trouble.

"He was only 14 then," Ros objected once he'd mentioned this to her over the phone. "He's eighteen now. Nearly a man. He's grown up."

Peyton was sceptical. "Mm."

Apparently the 'mm' said it all. Rosaline jumped on it immediately. "And he's very enthusiastic, very keen. He loves detective stories."

"This isn't a story, Ros. We'll be dealing with real, genuine danger here."

"Somehow I doubt that," she chuckled lightly. "But at least give him a chance."

Peyton rolled his eyes, more at the first statement than the second. Why did nobody take him seriously? He wasn't messing about here. He wasn't planning to solve the mystery of the missing next door neighbour's cat; this was a serious detective agency.

CHAPTER 2

"Mrs BOGGINS from next door has lost her cat; perhaps that could be your first case," Sherri suggested with a shrug as she placed the cups of tea down on the coffee table. The irony was not lost on Peyton.

"Right," he muttered, trying to keep the sarcasm from his voice.

Jack, on the other hand, seemed rather happy with the idea, his imagination already beginning to run away with him. "I bet he's been kidnapped."

"Catnapped," Peyton corrected him, staring at him blankly from across the sofa.

His sister, Ros, the mediator and arranger of their little business meeting, was trying her best to stay positive throughout. "Certainly worth a look into, isn't it? I mean, until you get your first proper case."

"That's another thing I can do, Mr. Kimble," added Jack, obviously planning to expand upon his already expounded list which included an apparent flair for making posters and fliers to advertise the business, being fast at running, handy in a fight, and the ability to pick locks. Peyton couldn't help wondering where he'd learnt that last skill from but he had to admit it might come in handy. "Finding new cases. I can do that. I mean, obviously they'll pour in thick and fast once we get our reputation built up but until then I can help us find new ones. I've got contacts. I even know a drug dealer."

"Why does that not surprise me?" Peyton sighed sarcastically.

"Oh shush, Peyt," Ros chastised him. "He's given up now, haven't you, Jack?"

"Oh yeah," he nodded. "I mean, I did used to smoke a bit of weed occasionally but...well, when I failed my exams it kind of...shook me up a bit."

Peyton reached for his tea and had a small sip, genuinely interested to hear what he had to say for the first time. "You regret it then?"

"Yeah, course I do," he answered

"And you think that's why you failed?"

"One of the reasons, yeah. That and just...generally messing around."

"What were you studying?" Peyton asked.

"Well, I was doing my A-levels but...I wanted to go on and study Chemistry."

"His teachers said he could have got into Cambridge if he'd applied himself," Rosaline tutted, shaking her head at him in despair. "But he never did. He was just like you, Peyton."

"Yeah?" Jack grinned at that and looked from his mother to Peyton. "Did you fail your exams too?"

Beginning to relax a little more in the conversation, Peyton rolled his shoulders then nodded his head. "Yes," he answered with a little sigh. "That's why I ended up working in a factory instead of being a doctor or a surgeon like I originally wanted."

"Or a detective," Jack added. "I thought you wanted to be a detective?"

"Well, I did. But everybody told me it was a stupid idea."

10

"That's what people tell me about all my ideas," said Jack. "But they're not stupid. I know they're not. People think *I'm* stupid, but I know I'm not."

"People used to think I was stupid too," Peyton admitted, the two of them inadvertently bonding without him even realising it. "They probably still do, down at the factory. I don't particularly speak to them."

"You've always been terrible at making friends, haven't you, dear?" Sherri teased him, patting his knee.

"Not *that* bad. I do *have* friends."

"That's alright, Mr. Kimble," smiled Jack encouragingly. "I don't really have that many friends either. I mean, I have a few, but not many that I get on with on a deep level, you know?"

Peyton looked across the coffee table at him thoughtfully. The kid talked too much; rambled, but other than that, he had certain things going for him. He was certainly enthusiastic, like Ros had promised; he saw positivity and good in everything, even getting excited at the thought of investigating a missing cat. Perhaps the energy and vitality that Jack offered would be good for the detective agency. Then there were his skills; IT and computers, fast at running, good at fighting, an able lock picker, a Cambridge Chemistry reject. That meant he was good with science. That could be useful.

"We'll have a trial run," he finally answered. "One week. See how we get on."

Jackson beamed happily, as did Ros. Even Sherri seemed pleased at his decision, despite her earlier scepticism over the whole affair.

"I won't let you down, Mr. Kimble," Jack assured him, standing up and offering out his hand to shake and seal the deal.

Peyton happily did so.

"Do you think we should refer to each other by our surnames now?" Jack asked. "You know, like Holmes and Watson? That would be cool, right? We could be Kimble and Chadwick. I think it has a certain ring to it."

"It's not bad," Peyton conceded with a small smile. "Like I said, we'll see how we get on."

"Where shall we start then?"

"Mrs Boggins from next door has a missing cat."

CHAPTER 3

"HE ALWAYS COMES IN for his tea at 6 o'clock. He's like clockwork."

"A clockwork cat. Awesome," Jack grinned and wriggled a little impatiently in his seat, eager for Mrs. Boggins to skip to the part where Speckles went missing.

Peyton wrote '6pm tea' down in his little black notebook, using the small blue pen he'd stolen from the bookies down the road. He decided that in future he'd ask Jack to take the notes. That way he'd be able to concentrate on other things such as figuring out whether the suspect was telling them the truth. Not that Mrs. Boggins was a suspect, and not that she would have any reason to lie about this in the first place.

"He's lived in this area all his life," she continued stating her case as to why she thought something terrible had happened to her precious Speckles. Peyton was struggling to take it seriously, but he tried his best. They had to start somewhere, after all, and Jackson's enthusiasm was rather infectious. "He's very streetwise. He wouldn't have got run over."

"You can't say that for certain," Peyton pointed out, as delicately as he could muster. "We do get some people speeding round here."

"He stays away from the road, Mr. Kimble. He rarely even goes out in the front garden. Just keeps to the back. We've never had any trouble with foxes or other animals. Cats have always been very safe here."

"Thank you, Mrs Boggins," smiled Peyton, closing up his notebook with a small but satisfying thwacking sound. "We're going to need a few recent pictures of Speckles, if possible, so that we can ask around the other neighbours and collect witness statements."

The idea of collecting witness statements in relation to a missing cat was slightly comical to Peyton, but he tried to make himself sound serious and professional. After all, he had an office now. It was official. Almost. He still needed the business cards; and he was planning to take Jackson up on his offer of designing them, as well as the posters and fliers to be distributed round Cheshire, and the text of the advert that he intended to put in the local newspapers.

As Mrs. Boggins hobbled off to find them some photographs, Peyton opened the notebook again and quickly scribbled Jack a 'to do' list then tore out the page and handed it over to him. "Think you can sort this stuff out?"

Jack cast his eyes quickly through the list and nodded. "Yeah, no problem, Kimble," he answered, already adopting the 'call each other by surnames' idea. "When do you need it doing by?"

"Oh…well…uh…" He hadn't actually considered that, and he wasn't sure how long it would take the lad to do it. "Next week?" he offered, wondering whether that sounded reasonable enough.

"Sure. I can probably do it sooner than that actually."

"Great."

"Here we are, here we are," Mrs. Boggins came bursting back into the room with a renewed energy, waving a fistful of

14

photographs above her head, eager to hand them over to the two new detectives. "Will this be enough? The most recent one was six months ago, but he's not changed a bit, although he does have a new collar. It's red now. The last one was blue."

"These will be fine, Mrs. Boggins," Peyton assured her, standing up to take the photographs from her. "Thank you very much. We'll get right onto this immediately."

"No, no, thank *you* very much, for finding my cat."

"Well, we haven't found him yet," Jack chuckled. "But we will do. Won't we, Kimble?"

Peyton sighed, then decided to join in with the surnames thing, taking it all in his stride. "Yes, Chadwick. We will."

CHAPTER 4

THERE WERE TWELVE houses on either side of the road, making for a total of twenty four and a possible twenty four suspects in the Case of the Missing Cat. Getting through every single one of them was a difficult and exhausting task, and took much longer than Peyton had anticipated. It was also, in the end, a rather futile task, seeing as everyone they spoke to insisted that they hadn't seen the cat recently and had no idea who might be responsible for his disappearance.

"Maybe he just decided to leave," Jack said glumly as they trudged out of the last house, late in the afternoon. Neither of them had eaten all day; they hadn't stopped. This detective business was harder than it looked.

"Why would a cat just up and leave?" Peyton shook his head. "It doesn't make sense. You heard Mrs. Boggins; she said he was perfectly happy."

"How did she know though? I mean really. Cats can't speak. You can't read their minds. How are we supposed to know what they're thinking or feeling?"

Peyton had to admit that Jack had a good point. Maybe this was just a futile, pointless case. How were they ever supposed to find a lost cat anyway?

He sighed and kicked at a discarded stone on the pavement and shoved his hands into his pockets, thinking.

"Chadwick...I think we'll call it a day...for today."

"Yeah? You sure? I mean, we can carry on, I don't mind."

"No, it's fine. We've worked hard. You need to go back to your mum and get some rest and something to eat. And I need to read through all these statements we've collected, see if I can put something together."

"We'll meet up again tomorrow?" Jack asked.

"Oh yes," nodded Peyton, trying to think of something constructive they could actually do the following day in relation to the case. "Tomorrow we'll....we'll...." Then suddenly, it hit him. Jackson had boasted earlier that he had contacts. Well, Peyton had contacts too. Ones that he needed to start utilising if they were ever to get further in this business. "We'll go and see my brother."

"Uncle Arthur?" Jack brightened up. "He's cool."

"Yeah? Cooler than me?" Peyton looked at him flatly, a completely serious expression on his face although in fact, he was teasing him.

"Uh..." His companion faltered, not wanting to answer the question. "Well..."

"Ha, it's OK, Chadwick...I'm just messing you around."

"Oh. Ah..." The young lad seemed to relax at that, and even managed a laugh. "So, we're gonna go see Uncle Arthur? What for?"

"See if there's been any reports of catnapping in the past six months. He'll be able to check the records for us, give us the details of anyone with any previous convictions for the same crime living in the local area."

"That's brilliant!" Jack answered enthusiastically, then stopped and frowned. "Wait; do people actually even get arrested for catnapping?"

18

"I...don't know. That's a good point. Well...we'll soon find out won't we?" He grinned and offered out his hand to Jack. "Thanks, Chadwick. You've done well today."

"I have?" He seemed pleased. "I'll crack on with those business cards tonight. And the posters and fliers. And the advert."

"Well, don't wear yourself out, lad. Just the business cards will do for now."

"Right you are!" Jack gave him a thumbs up and jogged across the road to make his way back home.

Peyton watched him for a moment, then chuckled quietly to himself and turned and walked off in the opposite direction, walking back to his own home just down the road, and next to their door to their new client's house, Mrs Boggins.

CHAPTER 5

IT WAS NICE to kick back and get his feet up after a strenuous day on the job and although Peyton had to field an array of questions from his wife about what he'd been up to and how much progress he'd made on their first case, he was still happy to be home. After a modest but enjoyable tea of soup and sandwiches, he sat down on the sofa and read through all the witness statements they had collected, trying to make sense of them, trying to find holes in the alibis and explanations, motives amongst the two dozen friendly and fairly ordinary neighbours that lived on their street. Why would any of them want to steal Speckles? He'd watched their faces extremely carefully during the interviews, or at least, as best he could whilst at the same time making notes. He was fairly good at telling when people were lying, or at least, he thought he was; and everyone they'd spoken to appeared to be telling the truth.

When his untidy scrawl and the depressing nature of his few findings began to wear him down, he opened up the laptop and went internet shopping instead. He had an empty office just sitting there in the heart of town, and he needed to fill it with furniture. They at least needed a desk each. That would be a good start, for now.

Sherri came and sat by his side, leaning her head on his shoulder and peering down at what he was doing, having a good old nosy.

"Wow," she whistled, almost sounding impressed. "You really are serious about this, aren't you?"

"At which point did you think I wasn't?" he chuckled. "Yes, of course I am. I want it to work."

"This stuff for your office then?"

"Yup."

"Don't spend too much money, sweetheart," she said tentatively. "I mean….what if it doesn't work out…and you've made all that investment."

"It will work out."

"Is Mrs. Boggins even paying you for finding her cat?"

"The posters she put up round town are offering a £50 reward. We haven't actually discussed it in person but I'm sure the reward will be ours once we successfully bring home Speckles."

"Fifty quid?!" Sherri snorted. "That's hardly going to make you millionaires is it? Especially since you have to split it with Jack. That's £25 each."

"It's only our first case though, Sherri," he maintained. "It'll improve over time. We'll get better cases, for more money. Once our reputation spreads."

"How are you gonna do that then? Advertising?" she asked. "Is Jack doing all that promo stuff you talked about?"

"Yep, he's designing posters and fliers," Peyton nodded. "And…tomorrow…we're going to go and see Arthur. He's going to help us."

CHAPTER 6

"I'M NOT GOING to help you," Arthur sat on the other side of his desk; his arms folded across his heavily framed, thick chest, and shook his head. "I mean...I can't. I can't just...go handing you files from the police. It's more than my job's worth."

"Nobody would ever find out," Peyton insisted, almost pleading now. He'd been so confident with Jack that this would all be fine; he didn't want to end up looking like an idiot in front of him. He could already feel the silent eyes of the young man on them, darting back and forth between brothers as he watched their conversation like one might watch an intense Wimbledon final.

"You want a bet?" replied Arthur. "Everything that goes in and out of this police station is monitored. Thoroughly monitored. Believe me, someone would know. And then I'd be the one in trouble, Peyton, not you."

"Alright. Fine. You don't have to *give* me anything. You can just *tell* me. I'll remember."

Arthur gave a hearty chuckle. "You really are a persistent little shit, I'll give you that."

"Of course," Peyton smiled. "I'm your annoying baby brother."

"Catnappers, then?"

"Catnappers."

Arthur began laughing again, his chest shaking a little with the effort. He ran a hand through his already slicked back, but thinning grey black hair. "In a word, no. We haven't arrested any catnappers lately. Honestly, Peyton, what do you think this is?"

"What do you mean?" Peyton asked flatly, unsure what his brother was finding so amusing.

"I know things have been tough for you lately with losing your job and all that but...there's other work out there mate, and you'll find it. You just have to keep at it, you know? Don't get off the horse, as they say."

"I've got other work, Arthur," he mumbled. "I'm a detective now."

"I don't mean that. You've got to stop living in a fantasy world."

That was it. Peyton had had about enough of people not believing in him, of people mocking his decisions. First his wife Sherri, now his brother Arthur. What was so fantastically amazing about him becoming a detective? Why did everyone seem to think it was such a joke?

"It's not a fantasy!" He snapped, slamming his fist down on the table and making a lone paper clip leap rather impressively high into the air.

Instinctively, Jack's hand stretched forward from nowhere and caught the thing on its return back down to earth, he grinned to himself, then immediately felt disappointed that nobody had noticed his excellent catch.

The two siblings were too busy staring each other down over the table. Most of the time they had a good relationship, got on well, but of course, there was always the occasional brotherly spat.

24

Into the silence that had descended, the sharp, shrill ring of Peyton's mobile phone pierced the tense air between them.

He took it out of his pocket and looked at the caller ID. Mrs. Boggins.

"Ah," he smiled over at Arthur pointedly. "That's our new client." Then he clicked answer and held the phone to his ear. "Good morning, Mrs. Boggins. How can I help you?"

Her frail but currently highly animated voice came over the other end of the line, and as Arthur and Jack watched Peyton with interest, they both noticed his expression change, and a look of keen excitement, his eyes widening just as much as his smile as he leapt up from his seat and already made a move to put his coat back on.

"We'll be over right away, Mrs. Boggins," he told her. "Just sit tight. We'll be over right away."

"What is it, Kimble?" Jack asked eagerly once he was off the phone, standing up alongside his partner and putting on his jacket too.

"There's been a ransom demand," Peyton answered proudly. "Someone really *has* catnapped Speckles."

CHAPTER 7

TWENTY MINUTES LATER and the pair had made the trip across town to get back to Mrs. Boggins' house, where they now stood staring at the note that Peyton's neighbour had laid flat on her kitchen table.

'Five hundred pounds in the phone box at 6pm tomorrow evening or the cat dies'.

"It was pushed through the letterbox this morning," she told them. "Folded in half. I picked it up, saw what it was and....well...I called you straight away."

"That was the right thing to do, Mrs. Boggins," Peyton smiled at her encouragingly.

"We should probably use gloves before we touch it, Kimble," advised Jack quietly, nudging his shoulder a little. "So we don't contaminate the evidence."

"That's a very good idea, Chadwick," Peyton agreed. "Do we have any?"

"Actually, we do," his enthusiastic partner grinned and pulled out a pair of plastic gloves from his pocket. "I took the liberty of popping by the Pound Shop last night on my way home. Picked up a whole box of 'em. Figured we'd need them at some point."

Peyton had to admit he was impressed. He hadn't even considered things like wearing gloves. Apparently there were a number of factors he hadn't considered. He'd been far more concerned with getting the office all set up and the business cards and the promotional items, far too wrapped up in all that that he hadn't actually thought about the practical items they would need for their day to day detective work. Not for the first time in the past twenty four hours, he was genuinely glad of Jack's assistance. Perhaps they wouldn't make such a bad team after all.

"Excellent. Good job," he praised him as he took the proffered gloves and slipped them over his fingers. Then he carefully reached forward and picked up the note. "I very much doubt the catnapper used gloves to deliver it. He or she is probably not expecting to get investigated by a private detective."

"Yeah, you have a point there, Kimble," Jack nodded. "Most catnappers probably think they're going to get away with it."

"Most catnappers probably do."

"You won't let him get away with it, will you, Mr Kimble?" Mrs Boggins asked hopefully.

"Most certainly not," Peyton assured her, turning the note around in his gloved hands and examining it. "We should probably put this underneath a microscope, dust it for prints, that type of thing."

"Do you know how to do that?" Jack asked under his breath.

"No," Peyton admitted, equally as quiet. "Do you?"

"No, but I have a chemistry kit and a home laboratory, I'm sure we can work something out."

"You do?" Peyton brightened up. "Well why didn't you say something before?" He turned his attention back to the note, then cleared his throat and addressed their client again. "The handwriting is quite distinctly male."

"It is?" Jack was impressed. "How can you tell? You know stuff about handwriting?"

"I've studied it a bit," shrugged Peyton. "Like I said, I have always wanted to be a detective. There's certain things I've got a decent handle on as a result."

"That sounds promising then," said Mrs Boggins. "Narrowing the field, as they say."

"Yes, and we should have more information for you soon."

"How soon? By tomorrow?" The old lady looked as though her white hair was about to turn even whiter with worry. Peyton felt quite sorry for her, and he certainly didn't like the idea of giving these catnappers what they wanted. They were going to get to the bottom of this by the following evening and avoid her having to hand any money over.

"Of course by tomorrow," he assured her gently, placing a kind hand on her shoulder.

"So, Chadwick," Peyton addressed his assistant once they were back outside. "It's time to get our thinking caps on. What kind of person would catnap? Who would take a cat and demand ransom?"

"A not very nice person?" Jack suggested.

"But why Mrs Boggins?" Peyton continued. "Why not any other person who owns a cat or a dog?"

"I don't know. Because they know she's got money?"

"Has she though? She's a little old lady with a pension, and five hundred pounds is quite a decent amount but it's hardly half a million. Anyone could find five hundred pounds if they really put their minds to it; take out one of those pay day loans or borrow bits and pieces from family and friends. No, it's something more than that."

Peyton felt as though he was on a roll. He was getting somewhere, and there was something there, something just beyond his grasp that he couldn't get his hands on yet. But he would do.

"She's vulnerable then," Jack carried on throwing theories around. "She's a vulnerable old lady and that's why they picked on her."

"That certainly seems more likely, yes," Peyton nodded. "That would answer the question of why her, but not the actual motive itself."

"Well, the motive is money, obviously. They're asking for a ransom."

"What do they need the money for? Anything specific?"

"I don't know, Kimble. I guess you'd have to ask them," Jack grumbled, putting his hands in his pocket and obviously running out of ideas.

"And we will do, Chadwick. We will do. But first things first, let's go back to this home lab of yours and see if we can analyse the note."

"We can always ask Uncle Arthur for help if we can't do it."

"Hmm." Peyton didn't particularly pass comment. Considering the way things had gone between him and Arthur earlier that morning, he would rather avoid asking for his help for the time being. He would need to prove himself first, prove that he could actually do this detective business. Maybe then his brother would take him seriously and start cooperating with him on some of their cases.

CHAPTER 8

"I WAS CONVINCED he was running some kind of meth lab down there," Ros chuckled as she let them both in and showed them through to the living room.

"Mum," Jack rolled his eyes.

"Especially after he'd seen Breaking Bad."

"I wouldn't even know how to make that stuff," the young man grumbled, taking off his coat and throwing it on the sofa. "I'm not that good. Besides, it's only a few test tubes and random chemicals. Nothing special."

"Well, let's see if it does the trick for what we need," Peyton smiled encouragingly as Jack began to lead the way, opening up the door to the basement and jogging on down, the elder detective following close behind him.

The cellar was dark and dingy and quite small.

Jack reached for a light switch on a string that was hanging down from the ceiling and tugged it. A dim, bare bulb flickered on, illuminating the miserable looking workspace. There was a rickety decorating table with wobbly legs set up in the centre, and a single folding chair. On the table were an amalgam of different bottles and jars decorated with white labels which had the chemical names and symbols written on in black marker pen. There was a spirit lamp burner, a rack of dirty test tubes, a mask, and a few beakers and different types of equipment. It was, as Jack had warned him, just a crude set up, but it would do. It was more than Peyton had in his own basement, so he wasn't about to complain.

"So um...what do we need to do this then?" He asked, wandering over to the table and having a look at everything; being nosy.

"Er...iodine should do the trick. Crystals though, not liquid," answered Jack, beginning to hurriedly tidy things up, embarrassed of the mess. "And we need heat, and a beaker."

Peyton searched amongst the chemicals for the iodine, whilst Jack got the rest of the equipment together. "Here we are, iodine." He plucked it out from the bottles and put it at the front of the table near all the other items Jack had collected.

The young man took out a box of matches and sparked up the see through blue flame on the spirit lamp. He placed a beaker on the stand and then maneuvered it over the heat to warm it up.

"Where did you learn to do this then?" Peyton asked eagerly.

"Chemistry books," Jack shrugged. "I've got this book called 101 Awesome Experiments. It's mostly really simple stuff but yeah, some of it's pretty cool."

"What do we do now?"

"Well um...give me the note..."

"Put your rubber gloves back on," Peyton reminded him, getting his own ones out.

"Oh yeah."

Once they were both fully protected, Peyton removed the note from his pocket and handed it over to Jack, who proceeded to lean forwards and curl it around the inside of the beaker. It just about fitted in, although there was a part at the
32

bottom of the sheet of paper that overlapped with the top as the circle met, but they didn't think that would matter too much.

"Now we put a few drops of iodine in the bottom of the beaker," said Jack.

"Righto." Peyton unscrewed the cap and held it over their experiment, shaking it a little until some of the crystals dropped out and hit the bottom of the beaker. "Now what?"

"Er...now we um...we cover it up, and leave it for a bit. I think."

"You think?"

"Well, I haven't done this one since I was about 14 when I first got the chemistry set."

"And you've smoked a lot of weed since then," Peyton surmised, hoping that they'd got this correct.

"Uh yeah," Jack admitted, covering up the beaker with a plate and stepping back.

The two of them watched in intrigued silence for a moment, wondering if anything would actually happen. It was Peyton's clear eye who noticed it first.

"There! Look!" He pointed excitedly at the note, where some odd brown stains in the shapes of fingerprints had begun to magically appear on the paper. "It's working!"

Jack grinned, hugely pleased with himself. "Brilliant!"

"Let's wait a little longer," Peyton suggested. "See how it turns out."

And they did do. They waited a good ten minutes and watched in quiet amazement as the chemicals did their work, the fingerprints on the ransom note becoming darker and darker until they were almost a bluey black.

Then they had to wait a further five minutes for the note to actually cool down from the heat they'd been applying via the beaker, before they could think about removing it.

When they finally did, they saw a set of grubby fingerprints all over the thing. They knew that some of them would most probably belong to Mrs Boggins, but there would at least be a handful that were the print of their mysterious and elusive catnapper.

"What do we do now then?" Jack asked. "I mean, we've got the guy's prints, but how do we actually match them to anyone, find out who they belong to?"

"That's where my brother comes in," answered Peyton. Although moments earlier he'd been reluctant to ask his brother for any further help - at least until their reputation was established - now he was convinced that Arthur would be impressed by their rudimentary but effective methods of collecting data, and the professional manner in which they were conducting themselves. Perhaps, if they could go armed with some of their new business cards, that would help convince him even more that they were serious and dedicated about the venture.

"How did you get on with the business cards last night, Chadwick?" He asked his new partner.

"Really well, Kimble. The design is complete and I ran off one test print on ordinary paper. Came out looking nice. I can run them out on the proper cardboard now if you like? Then cut them up and voilà, our very own business cards."

"Excellent. I wouldn't mind having them with us when we go and see your Uncle Arthur again."

"Oh yeah, good idea," Jack nudged him and winked. "So he'll know we're serious."

"Mm, exactly. Although I'd quite like to see the design first; make sure you've got everything right. I mean, I'm sure you have," he added the last part diplomatically. "But, you know, seeing as I'm at your house anyway, I might as well have a quick gander."

"Oh yeah, sure, no problemo," Jack happily agreed, blowing out the spirit lamp and quickly clearing the experiment away now they were done with it. Then he led the way back upstairs and towards his bedroom where he had the designs all stored on his computer. "Maybe you could take him for a drink as well, Kimble."

"A drink? What for?" Peyton gave him a confused look. "Been a while since me and Arty went for a drink."

"Well then, exactly," Jack seized on the statement to further his point. "Perfect opportunity to go for a catch up then."

"Hmm, maybe you're right," reflected Peyton as he hovered over Jack's shoulder to inspect the designs, thinking it through. "Take him for a meal maybe. Nothing special, just Wetherspoons."

"Wetherspoons is good."

"Make it nice and friendly, talk about the old times, get a few drinks down him, and then gradually work round to the topic of the detective agency."

"Exacta mondo!" Jack pointed his index finger at him cheesily.

Peyton smirked to himself and nodded, liking the idea more and more the more he thought about it.

CHAPTER 9

AFTER MAKING ARRANGEMENTS over the phone and apologising to his wife for missing dinner that evening, Peyton spent the afternoon struggling to put up the extremely annoying flat pack furniture that had just arrived in his new office, then made his way into the centre of town to the local Wetherspoons at the agreed meet up time of seven thirty.

Arthur was Mr Punctual, as always, and was actually there ten minutes early, already supping at his pint by the time Peyton walked in and located his table in the corner. That was a good thing though; it meant Arty was nearly one drink ahead of him and already nice and relaxed; off his guard.

Peyton was armed with a pocket full of the new business cards, which he had approved earlier round at Jack's and watched as he'd printed them off on card and cut them up into handy palm sized mini adverts ready to be distributed to all their future clients and associates. Resisting the temptation to get one out just yet though, he allowed them to continue burning a hole in his pocket whilst he got himself a drink and sat down opposite his brother, grinning broadly and holding out his hand for a quick shake.

"Thanks for meeting up with me, Arty; I know it was a bit short notice."

"Oh, it's alright," Arthur shrugged and took a sip of his bitter. "What's all this in aid of anyway?"

"Not in aid of anything," Peyton fibbed. "When I came in earlier, I suddenly thought, well damn, I haven't actually met up with Arty in ages and now here I am coming into him at work and asking for favours. I thought it'd be nice to, you know; just have a decent old catch up."

"Well yeah, I couldn't agree more," his brother smiled. "We've both been far too busy the last few months. I mean, obviously I heard about you getting made redundant and stuff but...well...why don't we start with that?"

"Do we have to?" Peyton laughed. "There's really no story to it. Sam's really struggling at the moment."

Sam Royston, his ex-boss, was the owner and manager of the car factory where Peyton had previously worked. The plant was independent and one of the last few of that sort left in the country, producing less than ten thousand specialist sports cars per year and demand continually dropping. There had been talk of a buyout and takeover from Jaguar, but Sam had remained adamant that he wanted to remain in charge of his own business and he wouldn't let the "bigwigs" tell him what to do. That, however, had meant cutbacks.

"You were always his favourite though, Peyt. I mean, you used to be."

"Yeah, I used to be. Until Gordon Tate came on the scene."

"Ooh. Are you jealous of him?" Arthur teased, chuckling mostly to himself as he picked up the food menu to have a glance through and decide on something.

"No," Peyton scoffed. "I was actually relieved when he picked a new favourite. He stopped bugging me to take over the factory when he retired."

"He wants this Tate guy to take over now then?"

"Yeah. Gordon's a young kid, you know. Nineteen years old and really rather enthusiastic. Anyone would think he actually *wants* to work in a factory."

"Well maybe he does. Not everyone is a frustrated dreamer like you, Peyton. Some people are just satisfied with their lot in life. You never have been."

"No, because I always knew I could be something better," Peyton protested. *And now I have my chance.* He didn't say that last part, because he was still trying to keep the topic away from the detective agency for the time being, but he was certainly thinking it. "What are you having?" He asked instead, nodding towards the menu.

"Oh, I don't know," sighed Arthur. "I'm terrible at making decisions sometimes. Probably just the burger."

"Burgers are good here," Peyton nodded. "I'll probably have that too." He stood up and went over to the bar to place the order and pay for the both of them before returning to their table with another round of drinks even though they still hadn't finished their first. "So," he smiled as he sat down. "How's Helen? And Kelsie? Haven't seen them in a while."

"They're doing great. Helen's still at the same hospital. Working nights at the moment but you know how she loves the work."

"Yeah."

"And Kelsie's just started Sixth Form College."

"Doing her A-levels?"

"Yep. She wants to study English Literature at uni."

"I'm sure she'll do fine," Peyton said encouragingly. "She's a bright girl."

Arthur was frowning, gazing out of the window. "When *was* the last time we were all together?" He asked slowly. "As a family?"

"Christmas, wasn't it?" Replied Peyton. "Last Christmas round at Bennie's."

"Ah yeah, I thought so. Seems like ages ago."

"It's only a few months. Time goes quickly."

Bennie was their step-father. None of them ever called him 'Dad'. He'd married their mother Mary when all three of them had already grown up and left the family home, so he played no real part in their upbringing. He had, however, been more reliable and trustworthy than their real father, who had virtually disappeared off the scene altogether after the breakup of his marriage.

Peyton had always had good memories of his real dad, Colin, and he didn't like to think ill of him. He'd done his job; he'd brought them all up and dispatched them out into the world as moral, upstanding citizens who had done vaguely well for themselves. Perhaps he saw no real reason to stay in touch. He had made the effort initially, coming to Christmases and birthdays, but the atmosphere between him and Bennie had always been a little tense and he no doubt felt uncomfortable. Peyton had made enough excuses for him in his mind over the years but the fact was, nobody even really knew where he was anymore, where he was living, or even *if* he was living.

They'd half expected him to show up at their mother's funeral two years previously but if none of them knew his contact details to get in touch with him and let him know, then he probably didn't even realise that Mary had passed away. He was no doubt happily going on with his life thinking she was still alive. Arthur had tried to use the extensive search database at

40

the force to locate him on a number of occasions, but he didn't have a criminal record and apparently never seemed to gain one. He was a moral man, at least they knew that much.

As the burgers arrived, the two brothers got to talking about the previous Christmas and reminiscing over some of the amusing things that had happened; such as Bennie's dog knocking down the tree and the rubbish unwanted presents that some of them had received.

"Have you seen him recently?" Peyton asked casually. Arthur had always been slightly more sociable and better at keeping in touch than he was.

"Who? Bennie?"

"Yeah."

"No. Not since Christmas."

"What about Rosaline?"

As her and Peyton lived fairly close by, and had indeed lived together for a while, the pair saw and interacted with one another more often than Arthur did, and were fairly up to date on each other's business.

"I spoke to her last month on the phone," Arthur told him. "She was the one mentioned about you getting let go from Royston's."

"Ah, OK." Peyton had been wondering how he'd found out, but had presumed it was Ros anyway.

"How's Jackson getting on?" Arthur continued. "Ros said he was due his results soon. What was he doing hanging round with you at the station earlier? Not got him running round after you, have you?"

Peyton picked up a chip, dipped it into the tomato sauce and popped it into his mouth, pausing for a moment in the conversation. Perhaps now was the perfect time to lead things round to the detective agency. They'd had three drinks and almost finished their food. They'd made small talk, they'd caught up with one another, they were both nice and relaxed, and besides which, Arthur had just asked about young Jack. He could hardly lie.

"He uh...didn't do too well, I'm afraid. In his exams. Didn't get the grades he wanted to go to Uni."

"Oh, that's a shame," Arthur shook his head in pity. "What's he going to do then? Retake?"

"Er, actually no. He's got himself a job. Good prospects; exciting. He enjoys it. He's passionate about it. He's doing really well." Peyton had no idea at which point he'd become such an advocate for Jack's position in the detective agency, having started off as a complete sceptic who doubted that the lad would prove any use at all. Everything he was saying was true though, and he found himself saying them not only so he could try and sell the idea of the detective agency to Arthur, but because he genuinely believed them.

"That's fantastic." Arthur seemed really pleased. Peyton got the impression that smile on his face wouldn't last for long. "What's the job?"

"Well..." Peyton paused then cleared his throat. "You know how you asked me this morning what he was doing running around with me?"

Arthur's brow was already furrowing.

"He's my assistant," continued Peyton brightly. "My partner, in fact, in the Kimble Detective Agency."

"You can't be serious...for God's sake, Peyton."

"I am deadly serious, Arthur, and I intend to prove it to you."

At this point, he put his hand into the inside pocket of his jacket and produced one of the business cards with a flourish. Although they were homemade and cheaply done, they looked professional in their design and had been printed on glossy card. Jack had lived up to his word and had done a thoroughly good job on them. Arthur somewhat reluctantly took the card from his hand and studied it as Peyton carried on talking.

"We have an office in the centre of town. All fully kitted out with desks, filing cabinets and equipment, even a secretary." That part was a lie. "And we have our first client now, of course, Mrs Boggins."

"Oh yes, the case of the missing cat," Arthur muttered sarcastically. "How could I possibly forget?"

"A missing cat with a ransom demand, you heard the phone call I received in your office this morning." Peyton stared across the table at his brother, locking eyes with him as if challenging him to say it wasn't at least in the slightest bit interesting. "You're intrigued. Admit it. You've never heard of anyone making ransom demands for a cat before, have you?"

"Well, I'm sure it's probably happened but...."

"But not to you. I'm giving you the chance to work on the case of a lifetime, Arthur." It was hardly Jack the Ripper, but Peyton was doing his best salesman job. Maybe that's what he should have done with his life. Been a salesman.

"Giving *me*?" Arthur looked surprised. "You still want me to get involved with this? I already told you, I don't know any catnappers. We don't have any on record, it's not exactly the type of crime we - "

"We have his fingerprints," Peyton interrupted, a proud look on his face that grew even prouder when he saw the effect it had had on his brother. Arthur fell silent and closed his

43

mouth for a moment, looking all confused and baffled. Peyton found it quite amusing. He almost considered taking a picture to savour the moment at a later date, but Arthur recovered quickly and started speaking again.

"What do you mean you have his fingerprints?" He asked. "How?"

Peyton had come prepared. He removed some gloves from the pockets of his jeans and, silently, whilst Arthur was watching, confused, he put them on. Then, he reached into the inside pocket of his jacket once more, this time drawing out the folded ransom note. The dark fingerprint marks that had been left by their experiment were still very much clearly visible on the sheet of paper, enough that anyone at Cheshire Constabulary would be able to run it through their own database and hopefully come up with a match. He knew that if he'd had his brother on side earlier then he could have just got the police to do this in the first place and saved them the bother of using their little home lab, but the fact that they were able to do so and come up with an effective result was a win on their part and would surely go in their favour with Arthur. He would have to take them seriously now. They knew what they were doing, after all.

Arthur reached for the note, but Peyton snatched it back.

"Not without gloves, Arty, come on," he chastised him with a smile.

Arthur tutted but nodded in agreement.

Peyton unfolded the piece of paper and held it up so he could clearly see the handwritten note and the fingerprints all around it. Arthur raised both his eyebrows, studying it for a moment.

"How did you do it?"

44

"Simple iodine fuming," Peyton shrugged casually, as if it was all no big deal to him and his partner. "We have our own laboratory." He failed to mention that it was in Jack's basement and consisted of a few dirty test tubes and beakers. "All the latest equipment. Very well stocked." He decided to go overboard on his exaggerations. Why not, he thought to himself. He was on a roll.

"Interesting," Arthur nodded thoughtfully. He picked up his pint and drained it back, then stood up to go to the bar. "Want another?"

"Yes, please," Peyton smiled, handing him his empty glass.

He watched him walk away, staring at his back whilst he stood at the bar and ordered their next round, wondering what he was thinking. Arthur had always been so impossible to read.

"What is it you want me to do?" Arthur asked as he sat down with a heavy sigh.

Peyton ignored the question in the first instance, concentrating instead on carefully putting the note back in his pocket without it becoming contaminated or damaged. "What do you think of my detective agency, Arty?"

"I don't know, Peyt," he sighed. "It's early days for you, you know?"

"Of course," Peyton nodded, understanding. "I'm not expecting it all to fall into place for me immediately. I know there'll be hard work involved, and that it might be slow progress at first but...things are progressing smoothly and quickly. And professionally too. You should see the posters and fliers that Jack's been working on. Really spectacular stuff. And what about our little experiment? What do you think of that?" He picked up his pint of lager and raised it to his lips. He wanted Arthur to concede that he was impressed. He knew that he was; he could see it in his eyes when he'd first looked at the note.

"It was...well, it was good," he slowly conceded. "Not much of a science man myself but...I certainly couldn't do that. And it seems to work."

"Course it works. We have the catnapper's prints," Peyton grinned. "This case is practically in the bag. All we need now is.."

"All you need now is for the prints to be matched to someone on the criminal database and voilà, you've got your man," Arthur finished the sentence for him, obviously already guessing the direction the conversation was heading in.

"Exactly."

"That's if he's in the database. He will have had to have been brought in before, remember?"

"Oh, I know," nodded Peyton. "And of course there's always a chance that he hasn't but...still worth a look, isn't it?"

"And you want me to take the look?"

The two brothers stared at each other silently for a moment.

"If you wouldn't mind taking the look," Peyton eventually answered. "Then yes, I would very much appreciate it if you took the look."

Arthur smiled, then slowly offered out his hand across the table to shake Peyton's. "I'll take the look."

CHAPTER 10

IT WAS A SMUG, satisfied Peyton who arrived in the offices of the Kimble Detective Agency bright and early the following morning. He had arranged to meet Jackson there, an arrangement they would be sticking to every day from now on, unless agreed otherwise. 9am each morning at the office, to discuss what was on the schedule for the remainder of the day.

"Morning, Kimble!" Jackson called cheerfully as he pushed open the door with his shoulder, carrying two take out coffees for them both.

"Good morning!" Peyton cried just as cheerfully back.

"You're in a good mood," the young lad noted, putting the coffees down on Peyton's desk and pulling up one of the wheelie chairs to sit down opposite him.

The office was looking a lot more homely these days now that it actually had some furniture in it, although everything still had that fresh, plasticy 'new' smell.

"I am," agreed Peyton with a happy nod. "And so are you, by the looks of things."

"Oh, I'm just excited about the case," grinned Jackson, opening up the top of his coffee then raising the cup nervously to his lips as if worried about burning himself. He blew on it a moment, then took a tiny sip. "What are you so happy about?"

"The meal with my brother went exceptionally well last night. Which I should probably thank you for, seeing as it was your idea."

"Wining and dining him worked then?"

"Like a treat. He's agreed to help us out."

"Brilliant," he enthused, looking pleased with himself and the outcome. Then he paused, frowned, and hesitated. "So um...what do we...do now then?"

Peyton closed the notebook of interviews he'd been reviewing for the fourth time, then obsessively tidied up his desk – even though it was already incredibly tidy. "Well, there's nothing much we really *can* do. We've interviewed everyone in the neighbourhood. We've interviewed the victim. We've analysed the ransom note...Is there anything I'm missing?" The thought that he might be missing something annoyed him greatly.

"You don't think it's any of the neighbours then?" Jackson asked. "I mean, definitely not?"

"They all have alibis," sighed Peyton. "Of course, one of them could be lying but...I really don't see that they actually have any motive for the crime. And then there's the fact that the ransom requested is relatively small in the scheme of things. Everyone who lives on that street already has five hundred pounds. They wouldn't need to demand more by kidnapping a cat."

"Catnapping a cat," Jackson corrected him with a smile, taking out his phone and sitting back in the chair, relaxing for a while. He might as well, he figured, seeing as they were just waiting now. Waiting for a phone call from Arthur.

Moments later the sound of his annoying iPhone game filled the quiet air of the office. Peyton tried not to let it infuriate him too much. Jackson was a good kid and had been a big help so far. He turned to his coffee instead and stirred it around with the little plastic spoon.

"How's your mother?" he asked, trying to make casual conversation. "Has she been asking about the investigation?" It had been Ros's idea for Jackson to join forces with him anyway so he imagined she would probably be very interested in how their first case was getting on.

"Oh yeah, she's been asking a ton of questions," chuckled Jackson, not taking his eyes off the screen for a moment; the sounds of his game continuing on. "I didn't tell her anything though, obviously. Told her it was top secret."

Peyton stared up at him for a second, although Jackson wasn't looking in his direction. Then he gave a short, snorting laugh. "Well, it's not really all that top secret, Jack," he laughed, calling him by his first name and briefly breaking from their now established habit. "I mean, we interviewed everyone on my street so they all know about it. Your Uncle Arthur and probably a good few number of the cops he works with know about it. And besides which, it's hardly MI6 material."

"Well," Jackson uttered slightly defensively, looking up from his game for the first time. "I didn't want to be indiscreet." The phone made a loud beeping sound and he looked down again to discover he had lost. "Damn it...."

Peyton smiled quite fondly at the lad. "Whilst I admire your discretion, I'm sure it won't hurt if you tell Ros a few details about the case. Help satisfy her curiosity."

Jackson started up the game one more time and tried again. "It sounds cooler to tell her it's top secret though."

"Well yeah, I suppose it does," Peyton granted. "Maybe I should try that with Sherri."

"Ugh, I'll tell her tomorrow," shrugged Jackson, becoming absorbed in his phone. "She's out on a date tonight anyway."

"A date?" asked Peyton in surprise. He hadn't known that Ros was seeing anyone. "With who?"

"Oh yeah, this guy she's been seeing for a couple of weeks. This is like their...third one now I think. Third date. Ainsley Tate. I haven't met him yet."

"Ainsley Tate?!" Peyton nearly spat out his coffee.

"You know him?" Jackson glanced up in surprise, switching off his game and resting the phone face down on the desk. He picked up his drink again and cradled it in his hands. The days were getting colder now that winter was setting in. A hot drink in the mornings was an essential part of warming up and getting the brain in gear.

"I know him, yeah," answered Peyton. "I mean, not really well but...I've met him a good few times. His son Gordon works at Royston's Cars. He's Sam's favourite. Probably going to be taking over from him when the old man finally retires."

"Mum always told me you were the Boss's favourite."

"Yeah, I was. I mean, when I was younger. Then, after I'd been doing it for ten years or so I just couldn't be bothered to put the effort in anymore. I've never particularly cared about cars."

"Wow. Why would you spend your entire life doing something you didn't care about?" Jackson looked at him in quiet amazement.

"Yes, exactly," Peyton mumbled tightly, not liking to be reminded that he had effectively been wasting his years away. He should have had the nerve to break off sooner, to do his own thing. It was too easy to just trudge through life day to day; time passed so quickly anyway. Now he was just making
50

excuses. He rubbed his temple to clear his own thoughts and took a sip of coffee.

"Is there something bad about him or something?" Jackson asked, a worried expression on his face. "You looked like you were about to have a heart attack when I told you his name."

"No, no, nothing bad about him," Peyton waved a dismissive hand. "At least, not as far as I know. Just...wasn't expecting Ros to be dating someone I actually know. It's a small world, as they say."

"Well yeah, especially in Chester," Jackson snorted. "Hate this place. Always wanted out, y'know?"

"Yes. Well. Now we have the detective agency to concentrate on, things should be a little more interesting for you around here from now on."

"I hope so," he smiled. "I mean, things have been good so far. Thanks for taking me on. You have taken me on, right?"

"Yes, I suppose I have." That was the closest they ever came to any kind of official agreement or acceptance of Jackson's new position.

Peyton wandered off into his own thoughts, wondering how Ros had ever actually come to meet Ainsley Tate in the first place and how they were getting on together. Based on the number of times he had met the man when he'd come to collect his son from the factory and stood around chatting for a while, he'd come across as a decent enough chap and of relative intelligence. He had no idea what the man did for a living. The most they'd discussed was the weather, the football results and occasionally a bit of politics, whilst Ainsley had waited for Gordon to get changed out of his dirty car overalls.

It wasn't exactly a surprise in itself that Ros was dating. She had been fairly active on the scene since splitting with her husband, desperately trying to find someone to take his place and act as something of a father figure for Jackson. It was little wonder that in the end she had obviously turned to Peyton to provide that father figure, as she had never had much luck in the love department. Peyton, as her older brother, wanted nothing more than for her to find someone nice and settle down. She deserved happiness, after the hard time that she had been through. Her ex hadn't seemed so bad at the time, but to leave her and abandon his child gave echoes of their own troubled family, and that in itself probably unsettled Ros more than anything.

"Have you met any of the neighbours yet?" Jackson asked, breaking the comfortable silence that had descended between the two of them as they both sat embroiled in their own thoughts.

"The neighbours?" Peyton looked confused for a moment, until Jackson signalled with his thumb to the room next door.

"You know, the uh...the other people in the building."

"Oh right. Er....no. Not really. I saw one of them in the stairwell the other evening after I'd been putting up the furniture but other than that, no. I'm not even sure what type of people have offices here. I think they're all from other private businesses."

"Yeah, probably. They had a few labels on the bells downstairs."

"Well observed," Peyton smirked. "Can you remember any of them?" It was a bit of a test. Peyton himself had made a mental note of four of the names, but he wondered how many Jackson had taken on board.

"Er...." Jackson frowned and thought about it for a moment. "There was Dr Rivers MD....Katz Insurance...uh....a weird one,

52

Luminous. I thought that must be some kind of light company or something...." He shrugged and stopped talking.

"That all?"

"That's all I can remember, yeah."

"Interesting."

"What is?"

"I remembered four different names than you. Mr J H Patel, Frankland Security, Brigson & Co, and Stage Antics."

"Oh yeah, well now you've said them, they do sound familiar."

"Interesting though, don't you think?" Peyton leaned forwards over the desk a bit. "Our minds must work differently from one another."

"I guess so. Psychology was never really my strong point."

"That's good though, I think."

"What? That I was bad at Psychology."

"No, that our minds work differently," answered Peyton. "It means we complement each other as partners. We'll both be able to remember different pieces of evidence."

"Yeah, I guess we will," Jackson conceded with a thoughtful nod. "I suppose you're right, it is interesting."

Just then, the bright red phone that Peyton had installed on his desk began its shrill, sharp ring. They both stared at it excitedly, then Peyton picked it up.

"Kimble Detective Agency," he answered in a sing song voice.

It was, as he had expected, his brother on the other end of the line. He was the only one he had given the business card with their new phone number to. They wouldn't be getting any new clients calling them up just yet.

"Got some news for you."

"Do you need us to come in?" Peyton asked hopefully.

"No," Arthur quickly responded. He got the impression his brother was trying to keep him as far away from the station as possible which he reasoned might possibly be a good idea seeing as there was a chance he could get into some kind of trouble for helping them, although it would have been nice to have been viewed with respect by the other officers. Perhaps once they'd established themselves as respectable and effective investigators they would be made welcome. "I can tell you over the phone. It's not bugged or anything," he added sarcastically. "You were lucky this time, Peyton. We got a match on those fingerprints of yours. Seems your catnapper's got previous convictions."

Peyton had to suppress an excited squeal, although he did wriggle around in his seat with his eyes widening in joy, giving a gleeful but silent thumbs up to Jackson as he listened eagerly to what Arthur had to say. Jackson grinned and gave one back, realising it must be good news.

"His name's Connor Whitley. He's been in juvenile for theft and drug offences. He's been off the radar for over a year but that doesn't necessarily mean he isn't offending. And uh...well...obviously he is. Moved into catnapping it would appear. Probably to fund his drug habit or pay off some bigger criminals that he owes."

"Sounds like a realistic assumption," Peyton agreed. There was a reason why Arthur had moved to the top of his game at the Constabulary. He was good at what he did, even if he didn't have as much imagination as Peyton.

"I can give you his address if you like," grumbled Arthur. "But you do realise you can't just go around arresting people. If you want him to be taken in for the crime then you're going to have to involve us."

"Well, you are involved, aren't you? You ran the prints for us."

"Unofficially."

"So um...how would we uh...go about...involving you?" Peyton asked carefully, sensing that there was about to be some cloak and dagger business going on, a matter that he was rather excited about.

Arthur sighed quietly then lowered his voice even further. The background noise in the office disappeared, as if he had just closed the door to give himself more privacy. Peyton waited, impatiently.

"Go over there. See if he's got the cat. Just....see. Look through his window or...round the back of the house or something..."

"I know how to be a detective, Arty," Peyton complained. He used to be like this when they were growing up together. Telling him what to do, telling him what he thought would be best.

"Just...listen, will you? Don't *do* anything. Don't make an arrest or get involved or even talk to him. Just establish whether he has the cat or not. If he does, you make a phone call to me and I'll sort out the rest."

"How?"

"I can say we had an anonymous tip off that he'd been seen with the cat. Then we can go round and catch him with it. That's all we need to make an arrest and for it to hold up in court."

Peyton was frowning. This didn't seem very fair at all to him. He knew that if he did it Arthur's way, then the police would get all the glory for having found the cat, arresting the culprit and returning the animal to its rightful owner. Mrs Boggins would be thanking Arthur, not him and Jackson. When in fact, it was them who had done all the work, who had made the breaks on this case. Why should the police get all the credit? And how were they ever going to get more clients and more cases if no one had ever heard of them, if they remained in the shadows never getting any recognition for the work that they had done? Surely there was another way to do this? He wasn't exactly sure how yet, but he would figure it out. For now though, he needed to appease Arthur that he would follow the rules. His brother was waiting for an answer.

"Are we clear? Peyton? Peyt? Are you listening to me?"

"Yes, yes, I'm listening," he finally replied. "That's absolutely fine. We'll do that."

"Good. It's Flat 4 of the Bromley Farm Estate on Parnell Square."

Peyton grabbed a pen and scribbled down the address then quickly thanked his brother and hung up, staring blankly into thin air for a moment, trying to think.

"Well?" Jackson demanded eagerly, keen to know what the conversation was about. "He knows who it is? We have a name?"

"Connor Whitley," Peyton answered flatly.

"Are you kidding?"

The response brought him out of his daydream.

"What were you saying about small worlds?" Jackson laughed.

"You know him?"

"Well. Sort of. I've bought drugs off him a couple of times."

"Why does that not surprise me," sighed Peyton.

"He lives on Parnell Square. Block of flats."

"I know. The Bromley Farm Estate. Number 4." He held up the scrap of paper. "We're going there now."

"Are we going to arrest him?" asked an excited Jackson, jumping up from the swivelly chair and already moving quickly towards the door.

"I think so, Chadwick," answered Peyton distractedly. "I think so."

CHAPTER 11

Peyton WAS STILL struggling to come up with a plan as he turned his car onto Parnell Square and slowed down as they approached the new council building that housed Connor Whitley's flat.

"How old is this guy?" he asked Jackson, who was sat in the passenger seat peering out of the window.

"I dunno. About the same age as me, I think."

"Does he live on his own?"

"No, with his mother."

Peyton put the car in neutral and pulled up the handbrake, sitting there with the engine still running and softly humming as he looked at the building next to them and considered their options.

"How well do you know him? Would he recognise you if he saw you?"

"I dunno. Yeah, probably. I should imagine so. It'd be bad for business if he didn't remember his customers."

"And have you ever seen him hanging around the Parklands?" That was the name of Peyton's street, and obviously the scene of the crime.

"Not as far as I can remember. Maybe. He's been round mine. It's only round the corner." Jackson and Ros had a pleasant 2 bedroom semi on Woolston Avenue, and both their houses were literally only round the corner from Connor's. A short walk.

"Give me your phone," Peyton suddenly said, getting an idea.

"What?"

"Your phone." He held out his hand for the device. "You get the internet on it, right?"

"Yeah, it's an iPhone, course I do," Jackson scoffed, taking it out and handing it to his partner as requested. "Most phones these days do, you know. I bet you still have an old Nokia 335 or something, right?"

"Don't be ridiculous," muttered Peyton, doing his best to navigate the annoying touch screen.

"Do you need help with that?" offered Jackson, full of sarcasm. "Old man?"

"Nope."

It did take him quite some time, but eventually, Peyton found what he was looking for, and leaned over to show Jackson the screen. A newspaper article about one of Connor Whitley's arrests, complete with a picture. "That's him, right?"

"Er yeah...that was a few years ago, I think but...yeah, definitely him."

"But you recognised him from this photo and you've only met him a couple of times?"

"Well. Three or four."

"Close enough. Can you take a copy of this photo? I mean, download it to your phone or something?" He handed it back over.

"Yeah sure," Jackson nodded, taking the phone back and doing as he was told whilst simultaneously giving Peyton an odd look when he put the car back into first gear again and began to move off. "Where we going? Are we not going in?"

"We can work this case ourselves, Chadwick. We can reach the same conclusions. Work backwards. We don't need the police."

Now, Jackson was even more confused. As far as he was concerned, they'd already completed the case. They knew who the catnapper was and they were here to make an arrest. Peyton wasn't making any sense. "But...but, it's him. We already know that. We got the finger print analysis."

"Except we can't prove it. Arthur can't admit to helping us because we're not official police and this isn't an official police investigation. He ran a background check based on our fingerprints and probably broke some kind of bureaucratic rule by doing so," Peyton swiftly explained as he navigated them back to The Parklands and the row of pleasant semi-detached houses where he lived. "The rest of that phone call was about him laying down the law about how this arrest was to happen. We're not allowed to get involved with it anyway. We just have to establish that the cat is there and then make a phone call to Arthur. He'll say that an anonymous call was placed to the police and then he can legally come to arrest Connor for his involvement."

"But...that's not fair," Jackson protested. "This is our case. We did all the work."

"Exactly. My sentiment exactly," Peyton took his eyes away from the road for a moment to point at him dramatically. "I mean, of course, I can understand where he's coming from. He's got to look after his own back, he's got to ensure a conviction and not have evidence getting thrown out of court as being inadmissible or whatever but...*but*...there has to be another way of doing it that can satisfy both sides' needs and...I think I've found it."

"What? How?"

"Our man Connor Whitley lives with his mother back there on Parnell Square. I can't imagine him being the type to mix with the posh folk down at The Parklands so...what was he doing there?"

"Well, he was going to steal the cat, obviously," Jackson shrugged.

"Yes, but how did he know a cat was there in the first place? And why that particular cat? How did he know about Mrs Boggins? How did he know how fond she was of her cat and that she'd actually be willing to pay the ransom?"

"You mean he's been there before?"

"He had to have been," said Peyton simply. "It's obvious, isn't it? Otherwise he wouldn't know about the cat."

"I guess you're right."

"How many other drug dealers and petty criminals do you know in Congleton?"

"One or two."

"Be honest. It's important."

"Five or six, I guess."

"Write them all down. Then look them up on the internet and try to get pictures. Do it now."

"Er, OK...OK..." Still unsure of Peyton's plan, Jackson opened up a document on his phone and began to tap in some names.

By this time, they had arrived at The Parklands and Peyton had pulled them to a stop on his driveway. He turned off the engine of the car and drummed his fingers anxiously on the steering wheel, waiting silently for Jackson to have finished his little task and thinking about how he was going to make this work.

"Are you done?" he asked, a couple of times.

"Almost," came the reply, again and again, until finally, he handed over the phone with a flourish and showed Peyton the photographs of four rather unfriendly looking chaps who had been arrested in the past couple of years on various charges. "I couldn't find all of them."

"That's OK. Four will do," Peyton nodded, pleased. "Four will be fine for our purposes."

"And what are our purposes? Are you going to let me in on this plan or just keep me in the dark?"

"You'll see," Peyton answered cryptically, getting out of the car. "You'll see soon enough. We'll try Mrs Boggins first. Can I keep command of your phone?"

"Er yeah," said Jackson, somewhat grudgingly. "Just don't...you know...break it or anything."

"I won't," he assured him, walking down Mrs Boggins' drive and knocking on her door. The little old lady answered a few moments later with her usual bumbling, bustling cheerfulness.

"Boys! Do come in, do come in. It's so lovely to see you both," she ushered them through to her living room. "Would you like some lemon cake?" she offered. "I've just finished baking it."

"Sounds lovely."

"No thanks."

Peyton and Jackson both answered at the same time, then looked at each other.

"We're not staying long," Peyton insisted, although still staring at Jackson.

"I'm sure we have time for some lemon cake," said the younger man tetchily, staring right back.

"Of course you do," Mrs Boggins gushed, wandering off to the kitchen to fetch it, along with a pot of tea, no doubt.

"Come on, Kimble," chuckled Jackson once she'd gone, giving Peyton a friendly punch in the shoulder. "Lemon cake's my favourite. We're not in a hurry, are we?"

"Oh, I suppose not," Peyton sighed, relenting to the stomach of his partner. He was quite hungry himself though actually, he realised at that moment. He'd rushed out of the house early that morning, wanting to get to the office to study his notes again and think about the case. He'd not actually had chance to eat, as of yet.

When the lemon cake did come a couple of minutes later, both he and Jackson were sat on the sofa and dug in to the tasty treat just as eagerly as the other.

"I have some photographs to show you," Peyton mumbled with his mouth full, then struggled to swallow it down first before speaking again, picking up the tea and washing it back. "I have some photographs to show you," he repeated, clearer this time. "Chadwick and I eliminated everyone on this street as a potential suspect in the catnap," he began to explain. "So we drew up a list of other possible culprits, of known criminals operating in the area that Chadwick had heard of. He knows quite a few criminals."

"Oy," Jackson protested, nudging Peyton in the knee. "You're making me sound like a right scumbag, Kimble."

"I knew one or two as well, of course," Peyton hurriedly added, lying to make Jackson feel better about himself. "And between us, we came up with a list. We realised that the culprit must have been here before otherwise he wouldn't have

64

known about your cat, so we've brought some pictures of the potential suspects to show you, see if you recognise any of them."

"Ooh, well that's a good idea," Mrs Boggins gave a nod of approval, cradling her cup of tea in her lap and shifting her weight slightly from one bum cheek to the other. "Let me see them then."

Peyton stood up and, brandishing the phone like a weapon, went to sit next to her on the opposite sofa, swiping his finger across the screen as he showed her one picture after the next. To each, she solemnly shook her head, even, disappointingly, the one of Connor Whitley. This didn't faze Peyton too much though. They still had several neighbours left to go and after finishing up his tea and lemon cake, it was time to move on and continue their rounds. He hurried Jackson along, quite sure that the young lad would have stayed for another piece of cake, but as soon as they got out of the door, he was back in detective mode too, and eager again.

"He can't have gone very far," he mused. "I mean, if he knew about Mrs Boggins cat then he probably didn't wander very far down the street, y'know? Otherwise he might have decided to hit on a different cat. Or a dog."

"That's decent enough reasoning," Peyton nodded, going to Mrs Boggins' next-door neighbour, the Thompson family.

There, they had the same result, although Mr Thompson was at work and couldn't give his verification on the photographs. They promised they would come back later that evening if they couldn't get any results, although Peyton was still hopeful they would get their match before that.

And two houses later, his hopes become reality at the home of Jess and Eddie Booth. Although both of them claimed they had never seen any of the suspects before, it was instantly clear to Peyton that Eddie Booth was lying. He had recognised the picture of their man, Connor Whitley. He wasn't exactly sure why he would lie about it, at that moment in time, but he definitely had. He'd seen it in his facial expression, in his body language, even in his tone of voice and the quick, paranoid way that he had answered 'no', then tried to make an excuse that he was very busy. He wanted to get them both out of the house. That was fine with Peyton. He needed to have a word with his partner anyway.

"Did you see that?" he said excitedly, once they were outside.

"See what?" Jackson asked blankly. Clearly he hadn't seen a thing.

"Eddie was lying. It was obvious!"

"Was it? Oh, I've never been very good at things like that. My mum says I have Asperger's. I can't read emotions and stuff." He shrugged.

"Well, maybe you do, I don't know. Anyway, he was definitely lying." He grabbed Jackson's arm in his excitement.

"Ow!" The lad protested, pulling it away. "So, he knows Connor Whitley then? I mean, that is who he recognised, right? Not any of the other guys?"

"Of course that was who he recognised. The other guys were just put there to add credence to our story. None of them had anything to do with it."

"Yeah, I know that. I get it. I was just checking."

"Yes, he recognised Connor. But how? And why didn't he want to admit it? Has he got something to do with the crime?"

"I thought you'd ruled everyone out round here."

"Well, I had, but...now..." He frowned, stumped for a moment.

"Maybe he just bought some weed off the guy and he doesn't want his wife to know he smokes a bit of grass now and again," Jackson suggested casually.

"Chadwick, that's perfect!" Peyton cried. "You're a genius!"

"Always knew I was."

"Now we just have to convince him to tell us. Need to get him on his own. Away from his wife."

"Maybe I could ask his wife some questions in the other room whilst you get to talk to him?"

"That might work. Except, he doesn't particularly want us there. Not to worry. We'll just have to insist." And with that, he marched right up to the door again and rang the bell. He was quite relieved when Jess came to the door instead of Eddie.

"Sorry to bother you again, Mrs Booth," he smiled, all sweetness and light. She'd been nice and cooperative, he was sure she wouldn't mind. "My partner here has just thought of another couple of quick questions. It really won't take that much more of your time, I promise." He hoped Jackson could think on his feet and come up with the questions he'd just mentioned.

"Oh. Oh, OK...no, that's fine," she smiled back and nodded, opening up the door to let them in.

"I wouldn't mind another cup of tea," Jackson said cheekily, indicating towards the kitchen and obviously trying to get Mrs Booth to take him in there so they could talk whilst she made it and Peyton could get Eddie alone in the living room.

"Of course. I'll go make you one."

"I'll give you a hand." It was more of a statement than an offer, and he followed her into the kitchen.

Peyton stood in the hallway and watched them go for a moment, then hurriedly dashed through the living room door. He didn't know how much time he would have before Jackson came back; how long he would be able to successfully stall Mrs Booth with their fake questions. He had to be as quick as possible.

"Your wife is in the kitchen making tea with my partner," he stated, although it must have sounded rather odd considering two minutes previously they had been saying goodbye and heading out onto the street. Eddie turned his attention from the television and stared up at him in confusion and amazement.

"No one can hear us," Peyton continued. "So you can tell me the truth. I know that you know Connor Whitley. I suspect he's been dealing you drugs but you didn't want your wife to know. She doesn't have to know. All I need from you is the confirmation that he has been here; that he has been to this neighbourhood and this street. I will keep your name out of it. The fact is though, this man has kidnapped a cat and he is planning to kill it unless we do act now. You owe it to that cat to tell the truth."

The little speech seemed to have something of an effect on Eddie Booth. Initially, his expression was hostile, defensive. His mouth was even ajar slightly as if he was about to speak and protest his innocence once more, or demand that Peyton leave his house immediately because he was so busy – watching television – but as the words continued streaming from the amateur detective's mouth and taking hold in Eddie's brain, something began to change. His features softened, he looked away; frowned. His hand came up to rub at the back of his neck, then he let out a heavy sigh and tutted, grabbing the remote control and randomly changing the channel.

"Just keep my name out of it," he grumbled. "Keep your promises."

"I will, I will, I can assure you," Peyton nodded. "So...so...that's a...yes then?" He had to hesitantly persist, wanting to get a definite admission.

"Yeah, I know him. It's...like you said. Nothing hard-core, just a bit of weed every couple of months or so, alright? No big deal. I just don't want Jess knowing."

"And she won't. How many times has he been here?"

"'Bout three," he shrugged. "Most of the time we meet round his or in town."

"And has he ever mentioned the cat?"

"We talked about Mrs Boggins once," Eddie admitted. "She was out on the street calling for Freckles or whatever he's called, and I said that she was obsessed with that cat. Just a bit of a joke. I didn't realise he'd...you know...go and do something like that."

"Well, he is a drug dealer, Mr Booth. And most probably an addict. Hardly the most trustworthy of folk."

"Huh. Suppose not."

"Thank you, though, for your honesty," Peyton smiled and offered out his hand as a gesture, sealing the deal. "Eventual honesty," he couldn't help but add. "And, like I promised, I won't say a word. As far as I'm concerned, we received an anonymous tip as to the cat's whereabouts." Using the type of language his brother spouted definitely made Peyton feel much more like a detective than he had done previously, especially now that he had effectively and successfully closed the case himself, without ever having needed to utilise Arthur's assistance to get the fingerprint analysis. Maybe if they'd done this originally, they wouldn't have even needed to go down to Jackson's basement and run the fingerprint test at all, but the entire exercise had been a useful and informative one in the different types of techniques they could use in the future to help solve their cases.

The admission came just at the right moment too, as Jackson and Jess had finished in the kitchen, Jess returning with a slightly baffled look on her face as though Jackson had asked her some rather odd questions, which he probably had. Peyton didn't like to ask. He just wanted to get out of there by then and drive over to Connor Whitley's again so they could rescue the cat and make the arrest.

"Ask me that question again, Chadwick," said Peyton to his partner as he walked them both back down the street towards the car.

"What question?"

"The one you asked me before."

"When?"

"When we were outside Connor Whitley's," he persisted, trying not to get exasperated. He was already expecting Jackson to be able to read his mind.

"I don't remember. What was it about?"

Peyton sighed. Explaining the question was going to spoil the effect of what he'd had planned, but he would just have to make do. "It was about whether we were going to arrest Connor Whitley or not."

"Oh right yeah," Jackson nodded. "I remember now. I asked you if we were going to arrest him and you said 'maybe' or 'perhaps' or something like that."

"I said 'I think so'," Peyton corrected him.

70

"Yeah, that was it."

"Well, ask me that question again." He unlocked the car and got into the driver's seat. Jackson jumped in and sat beside him, looking across at Peyton as they both did up their belts.

"You want me to ask you the same question?"

"Yep."

"OK um...are we going to arrest him?"

"We most certainly are, Chadwick," Peyton happily chimed, his response having now been set up for him no matter how long it took to actually get them there. "We most certainly are."

Jackson grinned, then laughed as the engine roared into life and they reversed out of the driveway back onto the street and navigated their way to Parnell Square once again. Peyton joined in the laughter, the two of them joyous and pleased with themselves. Their first case, and they were about to wrap it up neatly.

CHAPTER 12

"**W**HAT DO WE do now?" Jackson asked blankly, at a loss.

The two of them were stood in the corridor of Connor Whitley's apartment block, almost directly beside his front door, and they'd come up against their first problem. Because the young criminal lived on the second floor of the building, there was no feasible way for them to surreptitiously (and safely), look through the windows. The idea of a ladder had been muted originally, then scrapped as too dangerous and liable to draw attention to their activities.

Now, the detective duo had come up to the second floor itself to see whether there were any windows in the corridor that they could peek through; as it turned out, there was one, but the curtains were drawn and they couldn't see a thing. Peyton pressed his ear against the door and confirmed that he could hear the sound of the television, proving that at least someone was home. Either that or they had left the TV on when they went out. He paced up and down, silently thinking, then stopped and dramatically pointed at Jackson.

"You."

"Me?"

"Yes, you. Knock on the door."

"What?!" Jackson panicked. "Why do I have to knock on the door?"

"Because you have a history with him," Peyton hissed, aware that they needed to keep their voices down and Jackson had just almost squealed in the middle of the corridor. It was just a good job the telly was on loudly. "Knock on the door and pretend you're here to buy some drugs."

"Um...but I don't have any money on me."

Peyton dug into his pockets and brought out his wallet, handing over a fistful of notes. "Will that be enough? I've no idea what drugs cost these days."

"These days?" Jackson raised an eyebrow then remembered. "Ohhhh yeah, I forgot you used to be a stoner too."

"Shush, that was a long time ago. Now go..." He nudged him gently towards the front door then disappeared off down the corridor to hide himself round the corner where he could listen in whilst being safely out of view.

Jackson was left standing on his own wondering what on earth he was actually supposed to do when he knocked on the door and told Connor Whitley he was there to buy drugs. Did Peyton expect him to actually make the purchase? No, probably not, he most likely wanted his money back. They were there to confirm the existence of the cat. Maybe if he saw it, he could give some sort of sign to Peyton. But what? His mind was whirring as he raised his arm up to knock, then realised he didn't have to. There was a bell. He pressed his finger against it instead, and waited for any kind of response, fidgeting his weight from one foot to the other nervously.

It was his mother who answered the door, which made things even more difficult. What was he supposed to say now? 'Excuse me, I'm here to buy drugs off your son'?

"Er..." He faltered. It had been a long time since he'd done this.

"Can I help you?" the woman demanded, looking a bit impatient and fed up already. She probably wanted to go back to her TV programme.

"Right um...I'm here to see Connor," he managed to get out. "Is he in?"

"Yeah, he's in his room," she sighed and rolled her eyes, walking away and leaving the door wide open for him to head on inside. She seemed like the type of woman who was used to her son having visitors, which made sense considering he was a drug dealer. She obviously just left him to his own devices. Either she knew what he was doing and turned a blind eye to it, or she didn't know and didn't want to know.

Jackson hesitated for a further moment, glancing back down the corridor to where Peyton was lurking round the corner. "Kimble?" he called out in a whisper.

The man's head popped out, eager eyes shining brightly, soon to be followed by the rest of his quite short but agile body. At 5 foot 7, Peyton was the smaller of the two men, with Jackson a good few inches taller at 5 foot 10. It annoyed Peyton in many ways; he had always thought it best to have an assistant who was smaller.

"You go and see him in his room then," he instructed. "And I'll have a snoop around the rest of the flat."

"Alright, but his mother's in the living room watching telly so I'd avoid that if I were you."

"You're letting in a draft!" came the voice of the aforementioned mother from inside. "Either come in or shut the bloody door and piss off!"

"Well, that was an invitation if ever I heard one," Peyton quipped, nudging Jackson onwards.

The two of them entered the flat and closed the door behind them. Jackson gave Peyton a thumbs up, then began making his way down the narrow hallway towards the bedrooms. There was a bathroom immediately up ahead and then two rooms on either side, one of which was Connor's. He had been to the flat on one occasion previously, so remembered it was the room on the left, also given away by the fact that it was closed and had loud music blasting out from inside. He knocked, fairly loudly, so that he could be heard above the techno beats.

Meanwhile, Peyton was having a good old snoop around in the kitchen. It was only a small flat, barely big enough to swing a cat in, as the saying went; a very fitting saying too, considering the situation, although there was definitely no cat in here. With the living room out of bounds and one bedroom taken care of, he crept off after Jackson down the hallway and towards the second bedroom – the one that presumably belonged to the mother. He thought it unlikely that Connor would keep a stolen cat in his mother's room, but it was worth a shot. He just hoped Jackson was having more luck in the room next door.

As it turned out, he most definitely was.

After Connor had turned the music down and yelled out for him to come in, Jackson found himself standing in the young drug dealer's room with a cat mewing about his feet and rubbing up against his calves.

"New addition to the family?" Jackson smiled at Connor as he counted out some of the money Peyton had given him.

"Yeah, something like that," grumbled Connor. "What you after?"

"Oh, just a twenty bag."

Connor opened up his drawer and rummaged around amongst the bags of weed he had stored, tossing one over to Jackson in exchange for the cash. "Pleasure doing business again. I'll see you around."

Jackson took that as his invitation to leave. He didn't really know what else to do anyway. "Yeah. Thanks," he nodded and pocketed the weed before turning and walking out, just in time to see Peyton emerging from the bedroom opposite. He closed the door with a click behind him and spoke in urgent, hushed tones.

"The cat's in there. It's in there with him right now."

Peyton's eyes sparkled again with excitement. "Let's do it."

"Do what?"

"Arrest him."

"How?"

"I don't know. Jump on him or something."

"What?!" But Jackson didn't have time to question the finer details of Peyton's plan. The older man had shoved past him and pushed open the door, boldly stepping into Connor's room.

"Connor Whitley, you are under arrest for the abduction of Speckles the cat."

Jackson hurried in after him and closed the door, to stop either Connor or the cat from escaping.

"What the hell?" Connor scrambled to his feet and took a step back further into his room as he looked from one to the other. "No, this is my cat. Get the hell out my room. I've got a gun."

Peyton and Jackson exchanged glances. They hadn't taken weapons into consideration, which was foolish of them considering this was a drug dealer they were dealing with. They both took small, slightly nervous steps towards Connor, wanting to close in on him before he had chance to do anything. There was silence in the room, like some kind of Mexican standoff but without actual weapons, at least, for the time being. Then Connor made a sudden move, diving towards his bed side cabinet and reaching out with his right hand to pull open the drawer and grab something, the gun perhaps.

Jackson was the second man to move, and like a flash of lightning he had sprung himself upon the young dealer, grabbing hold of the extended arm and yanking it into the air whilst he flung a punch into Connor's stomach with the other, winding him. As Connor's knees buckled and he dropped to the floor, both with the shock of the attack and the pain of it, Peyton dived in and took control, placing his hand on Connor's back and pushing him further down to the ground before taking hold of both his wrists and yanking them up his back slightly.

Then the pair of them half sat on him, to stop him fighting and wriggling away. They were slightly out of breath, but full of adrenalin and utterly pleased with themselves. They had done it.

A phone call was placed to Arthur Kimble at Cheshire Constabulary and within ten minutes there were police on the scene to officially arrest Connor Whitley. No doubt the drugs they found in his possession would further add to his sentence of catnapping and extortion. As it turned out, Arthur's theory about Connor being in debt with some bigger, more dangerous dealers, had been quite correct, but he was in no mood to take pleasure from his correct deductions. He was far too busy being angry at his younger brother.

"You were supposed to observe and not intervene. To ring me," he chastised him. "Now what am I going to say about how you knew it was him?"

"Don't worry, Arty," Peyton just chuckled, slapping him on the back with one hand whilst he cradled Speckles the confused cat with the other. "I've got it all under control. I'll explain everything later," he assured him. "But right now, I have to take this cat back to its rightful owner."

Mrs Boggins was, needless to say, overjoyed. After showering them with more lemon cake, she got out her purse and gave them the reward she had originally promised - £50. As Peyton's wife Sherri had said when they'd first taken on the case, it wasn't exactly going to make them millionaires, but this was their first ever investigation and there were plenty more where this came from. He was sure that now this was over, the flood gates would open and the requests would come pouring in, especially after he gently suggested to Mrs Boggins that she could perhaps offer an interview to the local paper The Congleton Chronicle about what had happened and how two local private detectives had helped her find her stolen Speckles. The pleasant old lady was more than happy to comply and by the following day, the article was hitting the stands.

Arthur was satisfied with the extra work they had put in to ensure they wouldn't require usage of his fingerprint match, although he added that, "I hope this means you won't be bothering me to help you in the future."

"I wouldn't bank on that, Arty," Peyton grinned and once more slapped him on the back. "You should employ us to help out with some official cases, or at least throw some interesting stuff our way."

"For God's sake, Peyt, you really are trying to get me into trouble, aren't you?"

"What are family for?"

The two of them laughed, but it was an uneasy laughter on Arthur's part, and Peyton was unconvinced that he had him truly on side, as of yet.

The next step for the Kimble Detective Agency was to expand their advertising campaign. Now that a good number of people knew of their existence from the newspaper article, Peyton decided it was a good time to step up with the flyers and posters. They had already been cleverly designed by Jackson but had, until that moment, been sat in his room not doing very much.

The two of them spent an entire day going round the area, putting posters up in every window of every shop who agreed, and leaving flyers on the counters and worktops, occasionally even darting into cafes and leaving them on the table for people to pick up and look at whilst they ate. It was exhausting work, but fun and productive and, thirty six hours after their first case had been brought to a successful conclusion, the big red phone in their office began to ring. People had seen the newspaper article, the flyers, the posters. They had heard the rumours. They were interested.

Peyton wrote all the details down and promised he would get back to them within twenty four hours to let them know whether they could take the case on or not. Jackson was frowning at him in confusion once he had hung up.

"Why didn't you say yes?"

"Because we don't want them to think we're not busy," he answered. "We want them to think we're absolutely inundated with cases and that we have to pick and choose what we take on."

"But we're not."

"I know we're not, yet, but we will be eventually, and it's best to get used to working in that way now."

"Fair enough," Jackson shrugged. "That's actually a pretty cool idea. Treat 'em mean, keep 'em keen."

"Well, we're not treating them mean," said Peyton. "If I'm being honest, I'll probably call them back in an hour and tell them we'll take it." He laughed.

"What is it anyway?"

"Missing dog."

"Oh." Jackson pulled a face. "Are all our cases going to be missing animals?"

"I hope not," sighed Peyton. "I suppose we've already proven that we're good with them. We just need to build our reputation in other areas too."

The phone burst into life again.

"Wow," grinned Jackson. "Two in two minutes, that's brilliant, right?"

"I know," Peyton grinned back, equally as excited. "I wonder what this will be, a missing parrot?" He joked, then picked up the phone and cleared his throat, adopting his 'professional' voice. "Good morning, Kimble Detective Agency..."

Jackson waited eagerly, listening to the one sided conversation.

"Er...well, yes...he's right here..." Peyton was saying, confused. He frowned and offered the phone out towards Jackson. "It's um, it's for you. Apparently."

Jackson was just as surprised as Peyton was, but he took the phone and pressed it to his ear. "Hello?"

Now it was Peyton's turn to have to wait, resting his elbows up on the desk and leaning in, watching Jackson's face and trying to read it, wondering who would be calling him on their work telephone and for what reason.

"Oh..." he said to the other person. "Well that's...that's odd, yeah. I mean, she was fine this morning when I left so...yeah...no, I don't know...I'll try her mobile...yeah, OK...yeah, I will do...thanks for letting me know...thanks...bye..." He removed the phone from his temple and gently replaced it back down, hanging up.

"What is it?" Peyton eagerly asked. He could see from Jackson's expression that he was worried, that he'd had bad news of some kind. "Is everything alright? What is it?" The young man wasn't even answering initially, like he was in some sort of daze.

"I don't know," he eventually responded, shaking his head then raising up his eyes to meet Peyton's. "That was the office where my Mum works. Apparently she didn't go in this morning and they can't reach her on the telephone."

Peyton's heart skipped a beat, immediately worried about his sister. "That's odd. Has she been sick recently?"

"No, that's what they were just asking me but...well...like I told them, she's been perfectly fine, she was fine when I left this morning. No indication that she wasn't going to go in."

"Your mum works hard, always has done," Peyton told him. "She hardly ever calls in sick unless she literally can't get out of bed."

"I know, I know."

"And she would have called. She would have called them and let them know, she wouldn't just...leave them hanging."

"Well exactly," Jackson nodded. "That's what they were saying. It's very out of character." He was already taking out his mobile phone and trying to call her, apparently with no success. "Mobile's going straight through to voicemail too."

"Something's wrong," Peyton shook his head, getting a bad feeling. He jumped to his feet and grabbed his coat. "Let's just go round there."

Jackson didn't have to be told twice. Within less than a minute they were both dashing out the door of their office and scrambling into Peyton's car. The case of the missing dog could wait. This was much more important.

CHAPTER 13

WOOLSTON AVENUE was quiet and peaceful. The majority of people were at work and aside from a retired elderly man out sweeping some leaves off his steps, nobody was out on the streets when Peyton and Jackson arrived. Number 24, the small but homely semi where Jackson and Ros lived together, was empty. No car was on the drive. A quick scout around the house confirmed what they already knew and suspected due to the lack of a vehicle. She had gone off out somewhere, quite possibly in a hurry judging from the way she failed to alert the office that she would not be in work that day.

"What would cause her to rush off and miss work?" Jackson scratched the back of his head, trying to figure it out.

"It would have to be some kind of emergency."

"Yeah, except she doesn't exactly have that many friends."

"Nice of you to point that out," Peyton muttered sarcastically. "But no, you're right. It would have to be a family emergency then."

"Except, we're her family, and we're both perfectly safe."

"There's Arthur..." Peyton took out his phone and placed a call to Cheshire Constabulary. As soon as his brother answered, he was tempted to hang up, having confirmed that the emergency was nothing to do with him, but he thought that, seeing as he was on the phone, he might as well ask whether he knew anything about it. "Do you know where Ros is?"

"Ros?"

"Yes, you know, our sister."

"Yes, I'm quite aware of that, Peyton," muttered Arthur. "Why would I know where she is? At work, I presume."

"No, she didn't turn up today. Just thought you might know something about it."

"No. Is she alright? Have you tried her mobile?" There was a note of panic in his voice. Arthur had always been something of a worrier.

"I'm sure she's fine," Peyton tried to calm him. "We're just tracking her down now."

"Keep me informed."

"I will do," he promised, then hung up and looked grimly at Jackson, shaking his head. "No luck from Arthur. He's perfectly fine, so the emergency's not him. And he doesn't know anything about it."

"Why don't we ask that guy over there?" Jackson suggested. He had been watching the elderly man sweeping up his leaves the entire time Peyton had been on the phone, and seeing as Ros could only have gone out recently, he wondered whether the man had been there at the time and seen anything.

"Good idea," Peyton nodded in agreement as the two of them wandered over to him.

Jackson was vaguely aware of who he was, although he was terrible at names and couldn't for the life of him remember. It was even more embarrassing when the person whose name you couldn't remember somehow managed to remember yours, which was exactly what happened in this case.

"Well, if it isn't, young Jack," the old man chuckled, ceasing his work for a moment to smile a goofy smile at them both. "What can I do for you?"

"Have you seen my mother this morning?"

"Oh yeah," he said immediately. "She rushed out about twenty minutes or so ago. Took the car. Seemed all panicked and in a hurry."

"You didn't talk to her though? You don't know where she was going?"

The man swept up another leaf then paused, a deep frown on his face. "Well...not exactly...but...she was on the telephone...she said something like...'I'll be right there, Ainsley'..."

Peyton and Jackson both looked at one another, thinking the same thing and saying it aloud at almost exactly the same time.

"Ainsley Tate!"

Peyton ran off to the car again and flung open the door, with Jackson hot on his heels. "Do you know where he lives?"

"Yeah," answered Peyton. "I dropped his son off there a few times when Ainsley couldn't pick him up." He roared the engine into life and spun off the kerb onto the street, doing a three point turn to get them back out of the avenue.

"What d'you think's happened?"

"We'll soon see."

"Must be something bad for Mum to skip work," Jackson speculated. "Are you excited? I'm excited."

"Trying not to be," mumbled Peyton, concentrating on navigating the road and remembering the quickest route there. "If something serious has happened it would be wrong of us to be excited."

"I'm excited," admitted Jackson again. "It's like a case, isn't it? It's like we're going out on a case."

"Sort of."

Just then, Peyton's mobile began to ring. He struggled to get it out of his pocket then tossed it over to Jackson for him to answer.

"Hello, Kimble's phone," he cheerfully responded, pressing answer without properly looking at the caller ID. He fell silent as he listened to the person on the other end of the line, then responded, "Why, what's happened?....oh my God, are you serious?...Wow, shit...yeah, OK, will do...thanks." He hung up.

"What? What is it?" Peyton demanded, looking across at him from the driver's seat. Jackson was slightly pale, his eyes widened.

"That was your brother. He's just had a call from Mum...requesting the police and an ambulance."

"Oh my God, who for?"

"Ainsley's son."

"Gordon?"

"Yeah," muttered Jackson, flatly.

"Why? What's happened?"

"He's dead."

CHAPTER 14

PEYTON AND JACKSON had at least a five minute head start on the police, and they got to the scene of the crime – or incident, or whatever it was – to find that they were the first to arrive. Leaping out of the car eagerly, they bounded up to the front door of the Tate residence and rang the bell and banged on the windows in equal measure.

A shaken looking Ros came to answer within a few seconds, immediately flinging her arms around Peyton's neck and hugging him.

"Oh God...thank God you're here..." Then she frowned and pulled back. "Wait...how did you even...how did you hear about this?"

"It's a long story, Mum."

"Because we're top investigators," Peyton shrugged with a smirk.

Ros slapped him gently on the arm, but managed a smile. "There's someone dead in there, no joking around."

"What happened?" he asked her seriously, dropping the smile, the three of them still lingering on the doorstep and talking in hushed voices.

"I had a call from Ainsley saying he'd gone into his son's room and found him dead. It...well...it looks like a suicide," she bit her lip and shook her head. "Poor kid. An overdose of some sort. Ainsley tried to get him to throw it up but...he was already gone."

Peyton leaned in and kissed her on the cheek. "Are you alright?"

"Me? Yeah, I'm fine. Thanks, just....a little shaken up. I didn't even get time to call in sick at work."

"Don't worry about it. I'm sure they'll be perfectly understanding once you tell them what happened."

Then she stood on her tip toes and looked over the taller shoulders of Peyton and Jackson with a slightly confused expression. "Where are the police? Did you come on your own? I called Arthur..."

"I'm sure he'll be on his way shortly," said Peyton.

"It wasn't suicide," came a gruff voice just behind Ros. The stressed and anxious face of Ainsley Tate appeared. He looked as though he'd been crying, which wasn't all that surprising considering the circumstances, but Peyton thought it was encouraging that Ainsley was able to express his emotions rather than keeping them all shut up inside as some men were wont to do.

"Yeah, that's the other thing," Ros added, almost apologetically. "Ainsley's convinced that – "

"I know my own son," he interrupted. "He was a perfectly happy young man. He had the world at his feet. He wouldn't do something like that."

"They say that about a lot of suicide victims though, don't they?" Jackson muttered, not too tactfully.

"Mind if we come inside, Ainsley?" Peyton quickly asked, not wanting to give the man chance to get offended by Jackson's somewhat ill-timed but well-meaning remark. The four of them were still lingering on the doorstep and Peyton

90

was quite eager to get a head start before the police arrived, if this really was to be their next case.

"Of course, Peyton, yeah," mumbled Ainsley. "I'll make coffee for everyone."

"Tea for me, thanks," smiled Jackson, eagerly stepping inside.

"Actually," said Peyton. "Could we um...could we see Gordon's bedroom? I don't know if Ros mentioned, but my partner Chadwick and I are – "

"You're detectives now. Yeah, I get it," Ainsley muttered. "But this isn't some kind of game, Peyton. That's my son lying in there."

"I know, Ainsley. And we'll treat him, and the situation, with the utmost respect. I promise you, we'll find out who murdered your son and bring him to justice."

"You believe me then?" Ainsley closed the door behind them, seeming surprised, but slightly suspicious.

"Well, that is what you're trying to suggest, isn't it?" asked Peyton. "That someone killed your son?"

Without needing to be asked, Jackson had taken out his little notepad and was already beginning to surreptitiously scribble things down. It was good when the young man was able to read his mind, Peyton thought to himself.

"That's what I'm saying, yeah," Ainsley admitted outright. "I'm not 'trying to suggest' it, I'm *saying* it. I mean, I *know* it was murder. That's what it was. And yeah, you can take a look, if you really think you can help."

"I know we can, Mr Tate," Jackson piped up, trying to add to the confidence they were attempting to instil in their potential new client.

"Well, who would want to kill Gordon?" came Peyton's next obvious and logical question as Ainsley led them both upstairs. "Does he have any enemies that you know of?"

"No. That's just the thing. I can't understand why anyone would want to. Everyone seemed to get on with him. He had good mates down at the factory. Sam adores him like his own son."

"What about friends outside of work?" Jackson asked. "Or enemies, obviously."

"He didn't really go out all that much. When he got home from work he'd be too tired and at the weekends we'd go to the football together or just laze about at the house. He wasn't one of these types to be off out clubbing."

Arriving at the top of the stairs, Ainsley guided them through to his son's room and opened up the door.

Gordon Tate was lying on his back in the centre of the small double bed. To all intents and purposes, it looked as though he were asleep, but the three men stood in the doorway knew better.

Peyton was the first to make a move, walking slowly into the room and approaching the bed. He took out a pair of rubber gloves from his pocket (he always carried them around with him now), and put them on, surveying the scene as he did so. Jackson followed suit, replacing the notepad and pen in the back pocket of his jeans and putting on some gloves instead as he walked up to the other side of the bed, watching Peyton for guidance and further instruction.

"If this is the scene of a murder, Chadwick, rather than the scene of a suicide," the lead detective spoke quietly, posing a question for the young assistant to ponder on. "Then what, exactly, should we be looking for?"

Jackson considered his options for a moment, then answered. "The murder weapon?"

"Well, yes, but we know it was an overdose..." He cleared his throat and spoke louder, turning to Ainsley who was still stood in the doorway. "Ainsley, how do we know that it's an overdose?"

"When I came in, there was a bottle of pills in his hand, with none of them left in it."

Peyton looked down at the bed again. Both Gordon's hands were now empty. "What's happened to the bottle?"

"Oh er...I took it out of his hand to see what it was...to see the label on it, y'know?" He reached for the chest of drawers that was up against the wall near the door, and picked up the bottle which he had placed on the top earlier. "Here," he handed it over to Peyton, who took it carefully with his gloved finger and thumb, turning it around in his hands.

"There's no label on it," he stated, studying the small, brown bottle.

"No. So...I don't know what it was he took. I've never seen that bottle before. All ours have labels on and, even if the label was removed, there's nothing missing from the medical cupboard. I checked."

"Interesting. He must have had it with him then, or...whoever killed him brought it with him," Peyton speculated, offering the bottle to Jackson, who popped it into one of the plastic evidence bags they now carried around with them. "What else do we need to look for, Chadwick?"

"Er, well..." Jackson sealed up the bag and stuffed it into his pocket. "If he didn't take those pills of his own accord then, someone must have forced him to do it so...er...we should look for signs of a struggle?" he suggested hopefully.

"Yes!" Peyton pointed victoriously across the bed at him. "Perfect." He crouched down and examined Gordon's hands. There were no broken fingernails or anything like that, which was what he'd been hoping for. None of the bedclothes were upset, nothing in the room had been turned upside down and ransacked. It didn't seem as though there'd been any type of struggle at all.

Whilst looking round the room he caught sight of the computer screen, which was all lit up and illuminated on the desk in the corner, opened up on a Word document with a typed up note on it in large capital letters. Even at that distance, he could make some of them out. "Suicide note?" he asked, nodding over at the screen.

"Yeah," said Ainsley. "That's the other thing. It just doesn't seem like him to me. The choice of language, I mean."

Peyton walked over and squinted at the note in more detail, taking out his phone to snap a photograph of it for their records.

'I AM SORRY, I JUST COULDN'T CARRY ON ANYMORE. I'VE BEEN DEPRESSED FOR AGES. I DIDN'T WANT ANYONE TO KNOW. I LOVE YOU ALL. GORDON.'

"Gordon wasn't much of an 'I love you' type. And I would have noticed if he'd been depressed for ages."

Three sets of heavy footsteps could suddenly be heard coming up the stairs, and Peyton knew immediately that the police had arrived, and would no doubt be annoyed if they caught him and Jackson snooping around and doing their business. He turned his back to the door and walked back over towards the bed, taking off his gloves as he did so. His attention was drawn by the empty glass on the bedside table. He realised that Gordon would have had to have had some kind of liquid to swallow the pills with, whether he was taking them on purpose or being forced. Was that the glass he used? Were there any fingerprints or residue? He peered down into it, just as the police came barging into the room.

"Are you two family?" the Inspector in charge demanded to know, squinting at Peyton and Jackson. He had a junior officer with him and one Forensics chap. Peyton was quite relieved it wasn't Arthur. Their little rouse would have been busted immediately.

"Sort of," Peyton answered. Ros was family, and she was dating Ainsley, so that wasn't exactly a lie.

"Well, we need everyone out now anyway, please," the Inspector continued, a little impatiently. "Sorry. Thank you." He stepped away from the door and then pointed towards it with a sweeping arm, paving the way for them to walk out. Peyton nodded, then did so, followed by Jackson, then Ainsley. The three of them went back downstairs to find Arthur comforting Ros.

"Morning, Peyt," Arthur glanced up in surprise when they walked in, but gave him a small smile. "When did you get here?"

"Well, we came straight over as soon as you rang us," said Peyton, not quite answering the question.

"Yeah, but how did you get here before me?" asked the baffled elder brother.

"Ah, batmobile." He winked.

Arthur shook his head slightly despairingly then dropped his arm from around Ros' shoulders and stood to his full professional height, preening down his jacket. "I suppose I'd better get up there and make sure they're not making a mess of things."

"It wasn't suicide, Detective Inspector," announced Ainsley.

"I'm sorry?"

"He was murdered."

"What makes you say that?" Arthur asked.

Ainsley repeated all the same reasons he had told to Peyton and Jackson but they fell on slightly less sympathetic ears.

"But you don't have any proof, nor any idea who would want to kill your son?"

"Well, that's just the thing. Nobody would want to kill him. He was a great lad, really popular." Ainsley had just inadvertently shot down his own argument.

"Hmm. I'll keep my eyes open but don't get your hopes up," said Arthur, making his way upstairs. Peyton got the impression that Arthur had already made his mind up before he'd even seen the scene of the incident.

It took them twenty minutes or so, during which the three of them remained downstairs. Ainsley made some coffee for them all, as promised, and a tea for Jackson, who never drank coffee under any circumstances. It made him on edge and hyperactive, apparently. Peyton was glad he'd sworn off drinking it. He'd hate to see Jackson hyperactive. The lad was jittery and excitable enough as it was.

"I'm sorry, Mr Tate, there's no evidence to suggest your son was murdered," Arthur was saying as he came back down the stairs. "There's no signs of a struggle. There's even a suicide note. Perhaps it's simply a case that you didn't know him as well as you think you did. Were you aware of his use of marijuana, for example?"

"What?" Ainsley seemed genuinely surprised; shocked. "Gordon didn't do drugs."

96

"Well, we found this in his drawer..." Arthur held up an evidence bag containing an even smaller bag of weed inside it.

Jackson stepped forwards from around the table and squinted at it.

"We found the relevant paraphernalia too, I'm afraid," added Arthur. "Rizlas, a lighter etc. And there's not very much left in this bag either, so he'd obviously smoked quite a bit of it."

"Well, he certainly kept that from me," Ainsley shook his head, amazed.

"It's not uncommon for drug users to become depressed, or even unpredictable, especially if he was already prone to that kind of condition. As I said, Mr Tate, perhaps it's just a case of you not knowing him as well as you thought you did. Once again, I'm sorry. A post-mortem will determine what he had ingested to end his life, if you'd be happy to agree to one."

"Of course," Ainsley nodded tightly. "I want to find out. But he didn't kill himself. I know he didn't."

"Was there any sort of bottle near his body?" the Forensics lady asked. "Or any pills or medication missing from the cupboard or their usual places?"

Peyton looked at Jackson, then at Ainsley. He knew that the police would most likely view it as stealing from a crime scene, but seeing as they'd already ruled this as suicide and that Ainsley had given it to them of his own free will, he didn't think they would have much of a leg to stand on. Still though, they'd probably want to take it off them so they could take it away and analyse it. He was torn. One part of him wanted to keep hold of it and say 'sod the police' but then there was another part that realised it would be better to keep his brother on side, and to be open and honest, and this probably wasn't the right way to go about it.

In the end, his morals prevailed, and even when Ainsley looked like he was fully prepared to keep quiet, Peyton held out his hand towards Jackson so he could give him the bottle. "Yeah, there was," he announced. "An unlabelled one."

"What are you doing with it, Peyton?" Arthur wanted to know.

"I gave it to him," Ainsley admitted with a shrug. "There's no label on it or anything. I was going to toss it in the bin, to be honest with you."

The bag was duly removed from Jackson's pocket and passed to the Forensics lady, who snapped on a pair of gloves and took out the item. She held the bottle to her nose, sniffed it, then peered inside. "Doesn't appear to be any residue. We can take it back, run some tests? Pills'll show up in post-mortem anyway, so..."

"So, you don't really need it?" Peyton suggested, slightly hopeful.

"What do you want with it, Peyt?" asked Arthur suspiciously. "Are you two playing at detectives again?"

"We're not playing, Arthur," sighed Peyton. "The business is really taking off actually and I'm sure if you decide not to pursue this case as a murder then Ainsley will be willing to employ us to pursue it for him." He was jumping the gun a bit here, he knew, but by the persistent determination of Ainsley to insist that something dodgy was going on, he guessed that the man wouldn't be willing to drop it so easily.

He guessed correctly.

"Damn straight I would," he immediately answered. "Someone needs to fight my boy's corner. I don't know what your rates are. Would a thousand cover it?"

"A thousand would certainly cover it, yes," Peyton quickly answered, trying to hide his excitement. Considering they had been paid a measly £50 for their last job, to suddenly get offered £1000 was a considerable raise.

"There isn't anything to investigate, Peyton," Arthur sighed. "If there was, we would have found it. It's a cut and dry suicide. You can't force someone to take pills and have an overdose without them putting up some kind of fight. He wouldn't just be lying there peacefully with no signs of a disturbance in the room whatsoever. And what about the note?"

"The murderer might have cleaned up after himself, or herself," Peyton pointed out.

"We'll dust the room for prints if that's what you want," offered Arthur.

"Yes please," said Ainsley. "Thank you."

"Can we keep the pill bottle then?" Peyton asked, being more direct about it this time.

"What are you going to do with it?" asked Arthur.

"I don't know yet. But you don't need it, do you?"

"You can't just come to crime scenes and take evidence."

"I thought you said this was a suicide? Is a suicide still a crime scene?"

"Yes. You can have the bottle back after we've tested it," he muttered grumpily, then turned and led the way outside. The police team followed him, leaving the four of them stood alone in the kitchen once more.

"Arty doesn't seem to be taking too kindly to your new venture," Ros chuckled.

"Oh, he'll come round," Peyton sighed. "I think he's still sore about the fact that we got all the attention for the last case when he'd stuck his neck out on the line for us running those fingerprint matches that we didn't even bother using."

"We didn't use them so that we could save his skin," Jackson protested. "He should be more grateful. I can't understand why they wouldn't just let us keep the bottle if they didn't need it."

"Arthur can't be seen to be too overly soft with Peyt though, can he?" Ros pointed out. "He doesn't want people to think he's doing him all kinds of favours just because he's his brother. He's walking a fine line and he has to be careful. You both do. You're not official police."

Peyton took a sip of his coffee and conceded defeat, for now, but there was still work to be done before they could leave Ainsley Tate's house that morning. Five minutes later, some police medics arrive to take Gordon's body away. It was a bad moment for Ainsley; having to say goodbye to his son, at least for the time being, and Peyton supposed it really brought it home to him that he was gone now, he was dead, no coming back from that. He watched the scene with a small frown on his face then took Jackson by the elbow and tugged him outside.

"Now's a good time for us to do some investigating of the surrounding area," he said to him once they were out in the fresh air. "Leave them to do their grieving and sort out the body."

"Yeah, I don't do well with death," Jackson admitted.

"Does it upset you?"

"No, it doesn't bother me at all. That's the problem. I can see that everyone else is upset and I know that I probably should be too, but I'm just not. I don't really care. And I don't
100

know how to comfort people or make them feel better. So I just sort of stand there awkwardly. Does that make me a psychopath?"

"What? No, of course it doesn't," Peyton assured him. "You're just...I don't know. Socially awkward. Have no empathy. Something like that. You don't want to murder people, do you?"

"No, that's awful."

"Well then."

"I do sometimes have dreams about it though. But that was only after I'd been watching Dexter."

"Maybe you should watch less violent TV programmes," Peyton advised him as they wandered round the side of the house.

"What are we actually looking for then, Kimble?"

"Things that the police won't look for," grinned Peyton excitedly. "They're already viewing this as a suicide."

"Well, all the evidence kind of suggests that it is," Jackson had to admit.

"I know. But that doesn't mean it's true. And if Ainsley is going to employ us to find the murderer of his son, then we have to start off by believing that there *is* a murderer of his son."

"But what will we do if there isn't? Just find a random person off the street and accuse them?"

Peyton turned to look at him.

"It was a joke," Jackson quickly added.

"Oh. Well yeah, I thought it was. Just making sure. All that talk about being a psychopath."

"I thought you said I *wasn't* a psychopa – ooh look!" He cut off his own word mid-stream when he spotted something of interest down on the floor, pointing at it excitedly with his extended left index finger.

"What?" Peyton asked, squinting his eyes. Maybe he needed glasses, he thought to himself. He couldn't for the life of him see what Jackson was all up in arms about at first.

"Here," the young lad dropped down to a crouching position beneath the window of the living room and pointed at two small imprints that had been made in the soft earthy grass.

"What is it?" asked Peyton again, bending forwards with his hands on his knees to look.

"You know I did have a job once," Jackson grinned. "For about a week, before I quit."

"How is this relevant?"

"Window cleaning. I hated it. But at least it's been useful for something. Look...someone's had a ladder up against this wall...here, and here..." He pointed out the two imprints with his finger.

Peyton's eyes widened, then he followed the trail of the imaginary ladder as it led right up to the window on the second floor. "That's Gordon Tate's bedroom, isn't it?"

"I think so."

"Someone had a ladder up against the wall to get into Gordon's bedroom. And out again."

"Our murderer then?"

"I think so, Chadwick," Peyton grinned and clapped him on the back. "Well done."

"Thanks." He beamed proudly. "Should we take samples of the mud or something?"

"I don't know. Can we do anything with the samples? Maybe find out what type of ladder was used?"

Jackson took out his iPhone and started taking a few snaps, then held his finger against the groove in the mud. "Would you say that was about an inch?"

"Uh...I think so. Shame we don't have a measuring tape or something. Wait, they'll probably have one inside." Peyton jumped up energetically and ran round to the front of the house again, almost colliding with the medical team as they slowly and carefully brought out Gordon Tate's body on a stretcher. He quickly schooled his pleased as punch features to look more suitably sombre and folded his hands neatly in front of him, bowing his head a moment as one might do at a funeral when the coffin was going past.

He raised his head, caught Ainsley's eye and gave him a small, reassuring smile, then waited until the body had been put into the back of the van before approaching him hesitantly, apologetic to bother him at such a traumatic period for something so apparently trivial.

"You'll get to see him again in the morgue, I expect," he said quietly, hoping that that would offer him some sort of condolence.

"Don't know how I'm gonna tell his mother," Ainsley mumbled, shaking his head. "She'll be devastated."

Peyton had never actually met Gordon's mother, and judging from the fact that Ainsley was dating his sister, he was presuming they had long since split up and were no longer living together.

"D'you still see her?"

"Not for the past three years. Gordon said he didn't want anything to do with her after how she'd hurt me."

Peyton looked at him expectantly, wanting an answer without having to ask. Thankfully, Ainsley provided it.

"She cheated on me. Broke up the family. She begged me to take her back but...I just couldn't..." He sighed. "I know she loves Gordon though. I mean, of course she does, he's her son. She always hoped he'd forgive her when he got a bit older. Never gonna happen now, is it? You know, I was adopted, I never knew my parents. I wouldn't wish that on anyone. Always told Gordon he should appreciate what he had, y'know? That he only had one mother and one chance and that he should go and see her. He wouldn't listen."

Although for the most part, Peyton was anxious and impatient to find the opportune moment to ask Ainsley for a tape measure, the part about him never knowing his parents did actually raise his interest a little. Sherri was an orphan. She'd grown up her entire early life in a children's home before getting adopted when she was seven. It was a tough start for her, but she made it through and found a great adoptive family whom she was still in touch with.

Besides which, there was his own family's secret. The one none of them ever spoke about. His parents had had another child, which they gave up for adoption immediately after he was born. It was before any of them had been born too, so none of the three siblings were even aware that this had happened, until Peyton had overheard his mum and dad arguing over it one evening when he was just a boy; with his father snapping at his mother to 'leave things in the past' and 'you know it was the right decision' whilst his mum sobbed and wailed about her 'little Ty', saying 'I just hope he's alright' and other such things. Peyton had his ear glued to the door, absolutely transfixed, his imagination enraptured by what he was hearing. Then he had dashed off immediately to share the information with his older brother Arthur. Later on, the two of
104

them had approached their father to tentatively ask about what they had heard, only to be yelled at to never mention that name in the house again and certainly not to their mother; to forget they'd ever heard it.

Of course, they may not ever have mentioned it again, but they didn't forget. How could they? It wasn't something they could just erase from their minds, especially not Peyton, who had heard it all directly. In later years, as he'd got older, he had made some efforts to try and track down this 'Ty', but it was nigh on an impossibility. First of all, they didn't know if Ty was short for Tyrone, Tyson or some other name, or whether it was simply 'Ty' on its own. Secondly, they didn't know the surname. Although their own surname was Kimble, that would have been changed when the adoption went through, and Ty would now be operating under his new family's surname, and what's more, could be living anywhere in the country, or indeed, the world. He didn't even know what adoption agency they'd used.

Later, he'd put Arthur onto the task too, and he'd used some of his police contacts and resources to do a bit more investigating, only to reach further dead ends until they'd both finally given up and basically forgotten all about it, or at least, pushed it to the back of their minds. They couldn't even find a birth certificate for him, even though they were sure he must have been born under the name of Kimble. Peyton began to doubt his own ears, and doubt that he'd even heard the name correctly in the first place. What if it was Si? Simon?

That was over fifteen years ago; the last time they'd tried to investigate it, and given up. Peyton had moved on with his life and so had Arthur. He was sure they both thought of it occasionally, but that was it.

Back in the present day, Peyton gave a sympathetic nod of understanding to Ainsley and grimaced. "Yeah, well...that's what kids are like, I suppose." Not that he would actually know that, never having had any of his own, but Jackson was near enough. He viewed him like a son, occasionally. Rarely. "They never listen."

"No, they don't," Ainsley agreed with a sigh.

There was a brief silence between them as they watched the ambulance carrying Gordon's body drive off, then Peyton seized his moment.

"Listen uh...I don't suppose you've got some kind of tape measure in the house?" he asked. "We could really do with one for the um...well...for the investigation."

"Oh right," Ainsley looked at him for a moment as if slightly surprised. "So you're um...you're investigating already then? You're not waiting for the police verdict?"

"Yes, I mean...if that's alright with you. Thought we'd just...crack on. The police seem to have ruled it as a suicide already."

"No, no, that's absolutely alright," he nodded. "The quicker you find my boy's murderer the better. I'll get you that tape measure." He smiled and then wandered off into the house to retrieve it.

Peyton was well and truly in detective mode by now, and he was already beginning to grow suspicious of Ainsley Tate. Certainly, the man had seemed upset at his boy's death but not *that* upset, and why was he suddenly now questioning whether he and Jackson were beginning the investigation or not? Had he been expecting them to wait? Was he reluctant? And if so, why? Or was he just reading too much into things? Surely, it was the right frame of mind that in a murder investigation, no

106

one is above suspicion, not even the people closest to the victims, or in some cases, *especially* not the people closest to the victims. Did Ainsley had a motive for killing Gordon? He certainly had opportunity seeing as they lived in the same house together, but then what were the marks from the ladder all about?

Tens of questions and theories were swarming through Peyton's mind at once as he stood on the front lawn and waited for Ainsley to return, which he soon did, brandishing the tape measure as promised and handing it over.

"What are you measuring?" he asked casually.

"Oh, I could tell you that, Mr Tate, but then I'd have to kill you," Peyton joked, perhaps not an entirely appropriate joke considering Ainsley believed his son had just been killed, but it was the best he could think of to stop him asking too many questions. They wanted to keep this investigation to themselves, and keep everyone else at a bit of a distance.

Pleased with himself and now armed with the tape measure, he went back round the side of the house to where Jackson was leaning up against the wall looking bored and playing on his phone.

"You took your time," he said once Peyton emerged.

"Yeah, well I couldn't just ask him outright for a tape measure; I had to pick the right moment. And put Ainsley Tate down on our list of suspects."

"We don't have a list of suspects."

"Then let's make one. And put Ainsley Tate on it."

"Are you serious? You think he might have bumped off his own son?" said Jackson rather loudly.

"Keep your voice down, would you? And...I don't know. We just have to keep an open mind."

"But why would he hire us to find his killer if he'd done it himself? Surely he'd be happy with the verdict of suicide?"

"Because he's entirely confident that we won't be able to find anything out...because he's playing the part of a grieving and angry father who can't cope with the death of his son and is looking for answers that aren't there...because he thinks he's being clever by doing so and is secretly having the last laugh...lots of reasons. Either way, he probably believes he won't ever have to pay us."

"Well what makes you think he *will* pay us then? Maybe we should have asked for an advance...money up front..."

"I'm not saying for certain that he's done it, I'm just theorising. And if he's innocent then I'm sure he'll pay us what he's promised, once we find the murderer."

"If we find the murderer."

"Of course we will, Chadwick. Let's try and be positive, shall we?"

"I'm trying my best. Still want me to put him on the list though?"

"I thought you said we didn't have a list."

Jackson grinned and took out his notebook, starting a new page. "We do now."

Peyton smiled back. "Yeah, put him on the list for the time being. We can always cross him off again later once we rule him out."

Having scribbled down the name, the pair of them crouched down again in the mud and, using their new tool, measured up the grooves of the ladder carefully whilst Jackson made a note of it in his pad.

"So...so...we should..." said Peyton, thinking aloud. "Well, it might be useful to go to some kind of hardware store, I

108

suppose...and measure up a variety of different ladders until we find one that matches. We should measure the gap in between the two grooves as well...so that we know how wide the steps are."

"Good idea," Jackson agreed, taking up the tape again and spreading it across the gap, jotting down the number. "There's something else we should do as well, Kimble."

"What's that?"

"You know that weed the police found in Gordon's room? Well, I had a look at the bag it was in and...he definitely bought it off Connor Whitley. He uses these distinctive bags with a little picture of a weed symbol on, y'know. I've never seen anyone doing that in this part of town before."

"Really? Interesting. Are you suggesting we have a little word with Connor Whitley then?"

"Well yeah, I guess so. I mean, if Connor sold him the weed then he might have some kind of an idea of what state of mind he was in, probably better than his father, seeing as his Dad didn't even seem to know that he was smoking it in the first place. People keep things from their parents, y'know, stuff that they might not mind sharing with others."

"Wonderful idea, Chadwick," Peyton agreed to it immediately. "I also want to talk to some of the people at Royston's."

"Royston's? Oh right, yeah, the factory..."

"Yeah. Those people worked with him day in and day out. They might know something."

"And what about the neighbours?" asked Jackson. "Should we speak to them too?"

"Certainly the one on this side," said Peyton, pointing at the house opposite to where they were standing. "They would have had an excellent view of the ladder and anyone operating on this side of the building."

"Although I guess if this happened at night then they wouldn't have noticed anything."

Jackson had made a good point, and whilst it was obvious that the murder – or suicide – must have taken place sometime after Gordon went to bed but before morning, as far as Peyton was concerned, there was no harm in asking anyway. They needed to pursue all avenues and cross things off their list if they were to get any further in the investigation.

Once they had shown their business cards and explained their intentions, the elderly, retired gentleman who lived next door was friendly and amenable to their requests, even inviting them in for a cup of tea, an opportunity which Jackson was only too eager to seize upon seeing as they had left their drinks half-finished in Ainsley's kitchen.

"This won't take up too much of your time, Mr uh...?"

"Lawcock," the man provided his surname.

"Mr Lawcock," Peyton continued, perching himself up on the breakfast bar next to Jackson and watching as their host made tea.

"Terrible about young Gordon," Mr Lawcock shook his head sadly. "Always seemed like such a polite lad."

"Did you know him well?" asked Peyton.

"I spoke to him on occasion, just to say hello and such like..." He turned and settled the cups of tea down on the counter in front of them. "He mostly kept himself to himself, but I'd see him coming and going as he went and came back from work."

"Did you see him go out much? Other than to work?"

"Not particularly. He went out with his dad to the football, I know that much."

Mr Lawcock was so far confirming Ainsley's story about Gordon's lack of a social life. He was, to all intents and purposes, a young man who was entirely focused on his work and his career ambitions, at the expense of everything else. But that didn't account for the drugs. What were they doing in his possession?

"Did you know that Gordon was a drug user, Mr Lawcock?" asked Peyton, raising the cup of tea to his lips. He glanced across at Jackson to discover that he was already writing all of this down; pen in one hand, tea in the other.

"Gordon? Drugs?" The old man looked flabbergasted. "Well, I never would have put him down as the type, to be honest with you..."

"The police found drugs in his drawer when they searched his room this morning," Jackson helpfully provided the explanation.

"Well...that is...quite, quite extraordinary..." said Mr Lawcock.

"I'm afraid it's true," added Peyton, cradling his cup of tea between both hands and trying to pick the right moment to move on with his questioning. "Actually, Mr Lawcock...the main reason we came to talk to you today was to ask you about something you may or may not have seen over at the Tate residence..."

"Oh yes? What's that?"

"Were you aware of anything going on late last night? Any kind of activity?"

"Like what?"

"Well...did anything wake you? Did you hear anything?"

"I didn't, I'm afraid," Mr Lawcock shook his head. "I'm sorry I couldn't be more helpful. I didn't hear a thing last night, and I'm normally a very light sleeper."

"What about earlier on during the day?" Peyton continued, playing around with the possibility in his mind that the murderer could have been hanging about in the area and waiting until it had gotten dark and Gordon was in bed to make his move.

"Well, the window cleaner came round, that's all."

Peyton and Jackson both looked at one another, their faces falling in disappointment. That would explain the ladders, and suddenly, the most exciting lead they had was reduced to nothing.

"The window cleaner?" Peyton sighed.

"Yeah, he comes round same time every two weeks."

"Does he do your windows too then?"

"He does everyone on the whole street," said Mr Lawcock.

"Thank you, Mr Lawcock," Peyton mumbled half-heartedly, drinking up his tea and slightly anxious to be out of there. "You've been most helpful."

CHAPTER 15

"DAMN WINDOW CLEANER," the detective cursed once they were out on the street again, annoyed that their theory had been, quite literally, washed away.

Jackson wandered round the side of the house and crouched down near Mr Lawcock's living room window, examining the ground. "Yeah, there's imprints here too," he confirmed, waving Peyton over to have a look, only this time, his keen eyes picked up on something that Jackson's did not.

"Those imprints aren't as deep as the ones underneath Gordon's window," he said excitedly. "Which means..."

"Which means the ladder was at Gordon's for longer," Jackson answered.

"Which means our theory isn't totally scrapped after all...What if...what if the murderer knew that yesterday was the day the window cleaner came round...and that his ladder imprints wouldn't be viewed as suspicious?

The pair grinned at one another.

"Where's the measuring tape, Chadwick? We need to see if the ladder used was the same or different..."

"Good idea," Jackson agreed and hurriedly dug in his pockets for the tape. The two of them fell silent whilst Jackson very carefully measured first the imprints and then the gap, checking the results against the ones he had written down earlier. His eyes widened and he looked up at Peyton in amazement. "They're the same. They were made by the same ladder."

"Then we need to find out the name of this window cleaner and speak to him, add him to the list of suspects," said Peyton, already about to dash round and ask Mr Lawcock for the man's name when he thought of something else. "And then there's the drugs. That's a very interesting point too. Because, if Gordon really wasn't the type to do drugs – "

"- which according to Ainsley and Mr Lawcock he isn't."

"Then why did he have them in his drawer?"

"Do you think...are you thinking that...maybe someone planted them there?"

"It certainly seems possible, Chadwick. They knew the police would find it and knew how they'd react. They'd say that Ainsley didn't know his son as well as he thought and that Gordon was an unpredictable drug user who was depressed and took his own life."

"Which is exactly what they did say."

"So maybe we're dealing with someone who knows how the police think, knows how they would react to certain pieces of evidence."

"Then maybe they've dealt with the police before," suggested Jackson.

"Most hardened criminals have, at some point in their careers, dealt with the police."

"So, we're dealing with a hardened criminal then?"

"I think so, Chadwick..." Peyton frowned, still deep in thought and wondering what their next point of call should be. "How are we to talk to Connor Whitley with him in custody for catnapping?"

114

"Ask Uncle Arthur?" Jackson suggested.

CHAPTER 16

PEYTON HAD DECIDED to be upfront and honest with Arthur this time. If he was going to make a long term career out of detective work, then they would have to learn to work together. After ringing up and making an official appointment, they found themselves sat in Arthur's office less than half an hour later, with his brother having cleared a couple of other items off his schedule in order to see them, which Peyton made sure he was aware they were grateful for.

"How are you getting on with the investigation?" Peyton first asked, politely.

"Which one?" Unlike, the Kimble Detective Agency, still in its early stages, Arthur was used to being in charge of several investigations all running at the same time.

"The Gordon Tate murder."

"Suicide," Arthur corrected. "We should have the results back from the lab this afternoon, with regards to what it was that actually killed him. I suppose you'll be wanting to know too?"

"That would certainly be helpful," smiled Peyton. "Thank you."

"You really are pursuing the murder route then?"

"We are, yes."

"Have you found anything to substantiate these claims?"

Peyton quickly gave him a lowdown on the evidence and theories they had collected so far – the ladder imprints underneath Gordon's window compared with the imprints on the neighbour's and the issue of Gordon's drug use, or lack of it.

"Hmph...all purely conjecture so far...I'm afraid you'll need something more than that."

"I know," said Peyton. "Which is why we've come to you."

Arthur sighed and rubbed his left eye. "As much as I would love to help you out, Peyt...there's only so much I can do without it coming back on me. If you're going to start running round accusing people of murder, just remember you need actual solid evidence to back up your claims and – "

"We're not accusing anyone just yet, Arty. And this isn't a big favour. We just want a quick interview with Connor Whitley. Just ten minutes should suffice."

"Connor Whitley? What does he have to do with any of this?"

"We believe Connor Whitley may have been the one who sold Gordon Tate the drugs," Peyton explained. "In which case, he may be able to offer us some insight into his state of mind at the time."

"Hm. Well...you do realise he's in custody now?"

"Yes, of course...but if anyone can get us an interview, you can," Peyton smiled at his brother, trying to turn on the charm. "Like I said, we'd only need ten minutes. We can go into the prison to see him there...just put us in one of the visiting rooms."

Arthur sighed and drummed his fingers on the desk, as if mulling it over.

"Just think," continued Peyton. "If we're correct about this, we'll be catching you a murderer."

118

Arthur sighed again, then grumbled something incoherent under his breath. "Ten minutes," he said finally. "That's all I can give you."

"That's all we need."

"And you owe me another pint."

"I'll owe you two. How about that?"

CHAPTER 17

AS IT WAS to be expected, Connor Whitley wasn't particularly pleased to see either of them. The last time the three had encountered one another, Peyton and Jackson had jumped on him and made a citizens arrest that resulted in his incarceration on a number of charges; it was safe to say they weren't his best of friends.

"You two, again?" he groaned as the pair of them entered the room. Connor had been moved from his cell especially for the meeting, and taken to a small 'interrogation' room where he was placed down in a chair in front of a table and told to wait. He was still handcuffed, so that he couldn't attempt to escape, and there were two police officers waiting outside the door in case anything happened, as well as a CCTV camera set up in the corner, watching and recording everything that went on.

Peyton vaguely wondered whether the police would listen in on the questions they were asking him so that they could get ahead in the investigation before them, but he pushed the paranoid thought out of his mind and sat down. His brother's opinion most likely represented that of the majority of Cheshire Constabulary. Gordon Tate's death had been a suicide and they weren't investigating it any further. They probably had a wealth of other more open and shut cases to deal with that they deemed of higher importance anyway. They weren't interested in their interview with a small time drug dealer.

"Have you ever sold drugs to a young man named Gordon Tate?" Peyton asked immediately, getting straight down to it.

"How am I supposed to know?" Connor rolled his eyes. "I've sold drugs to a lot of people, mate. I don't exactly keep a list, nor ask their names most of the time."

"Have you got the photo?" Peyton looked at Jackson, who nodded and dug around in the inside pocket of his jacket for the recent photograph he had requested from Ainsley Tate just before the pair had left for their meeting at the police station. He slid it across the table towards Connor. "This is the guy," said Peyton. "Do you recognise him?"

Connor picked up the photo and studied it for a moment, then nodded. "Actually yeah. Yeah, I do. This dude picked up from me only a couple of days ago."

"It was definitely him?" asked Peyton. He and Jackson had muted the theory that the murderer had bought the drugs and then planted it in Gordon's room to make him look bad, but now that was apparently getting pushed to one side.

"Definitely him, yeah," Connor nodded. "This was the guy."

"Is he one of your regulars?" Jackson asked.

"Nah. Never seen him before in my life. This was the first time he's bought from me. I remember him cause he was all jittery and on edge about it, and I told him to relax. He said he'd never done anything like this before."

"He'd never bought drugs before?" Peyton leaned in across the table, deeply interested in what the young dealer was saying.

"I think that's what he meant, yeah. That it was his first time buying. Dude had some serious shit going down, I don't know what."

"What do you mean, exactly?" asked Peyton, using mock inverted commas with his fingers to repeat what Connor had said. "'Serious...shit'...?"

"Well he was all stressed out and stuff. And muttering to himself. Like, literally talking to himself. I think the guy had issues, y'know."

"What do you mean talking to himself? What kind of stuff was he saying?"

"Well, at one point I almost told him to get lost, cause he said something like, 'I'm gonna have to tell the police', and I thought he was talking about me, y'know? I thought he was some plant from the cops and that he was gonna go and hand me in or something. I got really freaked out. Then he was all panicky and apologetic saying he wasn't talking about me and that he just had a lot on his mind. I didn't ask what. None of my business. I just sold him the drugs and then left."

It was an interesting story, and one which only served to make the whole affair even more complex than it looked on the surface. What made Gordon Tate suddenly turn to drugs after apparently living his entire life without them, and what was he intending to tell the police? It became obvious that the young lad had got himself mixed up in something, perhaps something dangerous and beyond his own control. But what?

"That was all you heard?" Peyton asked. "Nothing more?"

"Pretty much. I mean, like I said, he was just generally talking and muttering to himself, but I only really paid attention when he said that thing about the police. I couldn't tell you what else he'd said before that. I was sending a text message at the time anyway, sorting out another deal. I made him wait a bit, just to check he was legit. I do that with all my new customers. Keep them hanging on for just a bit longer. If they want the product, they'll stay."

"Thank you, Connor," nodded Peyton, scraping back his chair and standing up.

"That it? We done now?"

"I think so. Unless you have anything else to tell me about this young man?"

"Nah, that's it. That's all I know, man. Do I get some kind of reward now, or what?"

"A reward?"

"Yeah, y'know, for helping you."

"I suppose we could get him something, couldn't we?" said Jackson.

"Like what?" asked Peyton.

"I don't know." Jackson turned to Connor. "What is it you'd like?"

"A chess board."

"A chess board?"

"Yeah. One of those electronic ones where you can play against the board."

"We can arrange that, can't we, Peyton?"

Peyton was thrown for a moment. He hadn't been expecting to give rewards to everyone who helped them, but if it meant possibly securing Connor's assistance in the future, then it might prove useful. "Only if you agree to answer any further questions we might have, about any of the clients you've dealt with over the years," he bartered with him. "Those electronic chess boards don't come cheap, y'know."

"Fine," Connor agreed with a huff, then managed to half stretch out his cuffed arms, extending the fingers on one hand for a shake.

Peyton leaned forwards and captured them, the two of them sealing the agreement. "Deal."

CHAPTER 18

NEXT ON THE AGENDA was a man by the name of Alan Morrissey; the window cleaner of Ruskin Road, where the Tates lived. Peyton had gotten his details off the Tate's next door neighbour Mr Lawcock, who still had one of Morrissey's old business cards with his address and telephone number on.

There was no one home when the pair called round just after two in the afternoon. As Jackson was only too happy to point out from his minimal but useful amount of experience as a window cleaner's assistant, those working in that field didn't just clean one street; they operated on a number of different streets, on different days, rotating between them all on a weekly or bi-weekly basis. It was very likely, therefore, that Mr Morrissey would be out on his rounds, cleaning windows, and might not be back home until later in the afternoon or early evening.

Peyton elected that the two of them should wait a while longer regardless, and announced that it was actually better that the man was out, because it would give them some time to have a snoop around the vicinity and see what they could find. Short of actually breaking into the house, there was very little they could actually do, but it was the garden that attracted their attention anyway, and the shed situated at the far end, which looked big enough to house a ladder or two.

"That's probably where he keeps all his equipment," Peyton surmised, and was proved to be correct when he peered through the dusty window to see a single ladder lying vertically across the ground. "Yes, there's definitely one in here...take a look."

When he turned and stepped back to allow Jackson room to peep through the window too, he discovered the young lad on his knees in front of the door, already beginning to pick the padlock so that they could gain access.

"Well. You don't mess around, do you?"

"We don't know when he's going to be back," he muttered. "Might as well act quickly and get this done with. Keep an eye on the neighbours would you, Kimble?"

Discovering that the roles had been somewhat reversed and that Jackson was the one currently in charge, Peyton silently did as he was told and stood next to his partner, keeping his eyes on the house opposite them and hoping the residents were all out at work too. Once again he found himself wondering where Jackson had learnt this dubious skill, but also once again thinking that he'd probably rather not know. Besides which, it was a useful skill, and one that, within five minutes, had gained them access to Mr Morrissey's equipment shed.

It basically contained all the usual essential items one might find in an average garden shed; a shovel, spade, gardening gloves, shears, a lawn mower, and of course, the ladder. The majority of people kept a ladder somewhere in their home anyway, for odd jobs round the house like changing awkward light bulbs and so on, but this ladder had been used for a very different purpose, so they hoped.

Jackson took out the tape measure and the two of them crouched down on the floor beside the feet of the ladder in question, only to end up disappointed. It wasn't a match.

"Well, he probably has more than one ladder," said Jackson hopefully. "And if he's out working right now, then maybe he has the one we want with him."

"In which case, we'll just have to wait until he comes home."

"What the hell are you doing on my property?" came a gruff, angry voice from just behind their shoulders. As it turned out, they didn't have to wait very long.

They turned round slowly to see a very annoyed looking six foot man brandishing a cricket bat and blocking the narrow doorway which was their only entrance and exit to the shed.

"Well?" he said, obviously demanding an answer. "How did you even get in? Break the lock, did you?"

"I picked it, actually," Jackson quickly assured him, as if that would make him feel better. "It's not damaged in anyway, you'll be able to put it back on again afterwards."

"Useful to know," the man replied, and then promptly took one step back and proceeded to slam the door shut.

"No!" Peyton managed to get out one single word of protest as he stood up and dived towards the quickly closing door, but by then it was already too late. The man, Alan Morrissey they presumed, had slipped on the padlock and clicked it into place, locking them both inside the dark confined space of the garden shed.

"You can stay there until the police come," they heard his muffled voice from the outside as he peered through the window to look at them. "I'm calling them right now." Then he turned and walked off. They heard his footsteps receding along

129

the gravel path that led him to the back door of the house, and then nothing. Silence.

"Well. This is just wonderful," muttered Peyton sarcastically.

"You could have told him we were detectives!" Jackson protested, standing up and having to lower his head due to the minimal height of the roof.

"I hardly had the chance to tell him anything, never mind that! What was I going to do, give him a bloody business card?!"

"Well yes! Maybe!"

"I didn't get chance! He just presumed we were burglars and locked us in!"

"I know, Kimble! I was there, remember! I saw it all happen, like, one minute ago..."

Their little outburst of an argument done with, the two of them relapsed into awkward silence again, trying to figure out what they should do.

"Well, we can't stay here until the police come," decided Peyton. "I can just imagine Arthur's face now."

Jackson tried the door, rattling it on its hinges. "How do you suppose we get out though? We're padlocked in."

"The window?"

It was hardly big enough for a dog to crawl through, let alone two fully grown men, but Jackson approached it anyway and had a little look. "Oh my God," he suddenly gasped.

"What?" asked Peyton. "Is it going to work? Can you get it off?"

But it wasn't anything to do with the actual window that had caught Jackson's attention. It was something going on outside. "Come here," he beckoned quickly with his hand.

130

"Come and look at this." He moved up a bit so that Peyton could stand at his shoulder and the two of them could share the limited view from the tiny window.

Over by the back door of the house, the patio doors were wide open, and three men – including the one who had locked them in – were carrying out items from inside the house; a vase, a picture in an expensive looking frame, a Blu-Ray player, a flat screen television.

Peyton and Jackson both looked at one another with widened eyes as the implication sank in.

"Then...that wasn't Alan Morrissey," Jackson spoke their thoughts aloud.

"No. I don't think any of those men are Alan Morrissey. And I don't think any of them will be calling the police anytime soon."

"Well then, doesn't that mean we're safe? We can just...stay here?"

"Safe? We're witnesses to a burglary, Chadwick. And they probably think we're rival burglars considering we picked the lock. What if they just...kill us? Besides, we can't just...sit here and allow them to rob someone's house. We're detectives. We're not going to be implicit in a crime by saying and doing nothing."

"Well yeah but, there's not very much we can do from here is there? I dunno. Except maybe call the police ourselves, but then you have the same problem of Arthur finding out about us being locked in a shed and knowing that we picked the lock to get in here."

But Peyton was already taking out his phone. If they had to call the police, then that was what they had to do. There was really no other option. They would deal with the consequences later. They had to do the right thing. As he brought it out of his pocket, something else fell out and onto the floor. Jackson bent to pick it up and hand it back, but he was immediately struck with an idea instead when he saw what it was.

"The business card!" he cried.

"What?" Peyton was already keying in 999.

"The business card, Kimble. The one that you got off that neighbour, Mr Lawcock. Alan Morrissey's business card." He swivelled it round to show Peyton the front. "It's got his mobile number on it."

Peyton paused. The pair made eye contact, then the detective grabbed the card off his assistant and began keying in that number instead. "Perfect, Chadwick...you really are helpful sometimes."

"Sometimes? Thanks," Jackson muttered with a laugh, until Peyton shushed him and held up a finger. The phone was pressed to his ear and it was ringing.

"Hello," came the voice on the other end.

"Hello, is this Alan Morrissey?"

"Yeah."

"You don't know me. My name is Peyton Kimble and I'm a detective with – "

"The Kimble Detective Agency, yeah I read it in the paper," Morrissey interrupted him before he could finish the introduction. He'd heard of him, then. That was good news.

"Yeah, that's it. Well, the thing is, Mr Morrissey, we came round to your house today to ask you a few questions with regard to a case we're currently working on, but unfortunately, we have since been locked in the shed by a group of three men who are, right at this minute, robbing your house."

"What?!"

"I'm serious. If you come round right now, you'll catch them at it. And you should probably call the police."

"I will do. I will do. Thanks mate." He hung up.

Jackson looked at Peyton blankly for a few moments in the aftermath of the phone call. "But....but what if...what if he comes round and the burglars attack him?"

"They won't do that," Peyton tried to insist, waving his hand, although now he was uncertain. "Besides, I did tell him to call the police."

"Do you think he'll call the police if he's a murderer?"

"Well, if he's a murderer he probably doesn't need the police to defend him from a rabble of burglars, does he now?"

Less than ten minutes later, he was proven to be correct. They heard a scuffle of feet, a loud smacking noise, a grunt, a cry, a shout, then more footstep sounds; only this time they were running away, receding into the distance.

The two of them were jostling and bustling over each other's shoulders the entire time, trying their best to see out of the small crack and find out what was going on. Apparently it was all happening at the front of the house, however, for they saw nothing, save for when a well-built man they hadn't seen before began walking down the alleyway by the side of the building and approached their tiny prison.

"In here!" Jackson shouted to him.

Peyton nudged him in the ribs. "I think he knows that, Chadwick. We did tell him."

The man remained silent as he arrived at the door of the shed, quickly releasing the padlock and letting them out.

"Thank you very much," Peyton nodded and offered out his hand. "We spoke on the phone. My name's – "

"Peyton Kimble, yeah. I know," grunted the man, taking Peyton's hand and giving it a firm, bone crunching shake. "Alan Morrissey. You said you wanted to talk to me about something?"

He turned and walked off, closed the back doors of his house, then wandered lazily around the front, leaving both Peyton and Jackson stood in the spot for a moment, staring at him in surprise with a dozen questions on their lips.

"What happened to the burglars?" Peyton blurted, desperate to know whether the sounds they had heard were really what they imagined them to be.

"Saw 'em off," grunted Morrissey without turning round to look at them.

Peyton and Jackson glanced at one another then and at the same time, set off scuttling after him, following him down the side alley and back to the front, where Morrissey began unloading his car with the ladder that was strapped to the top. He obviously had more than one then, as they had previously surmised.

"How?" asked Jackson.

"Broke one of their arms. Rest of 'em didn't want to stick around after that. They all ran away."

The eyes of the other two widened to the size of plates, and Peyton took a slightly nervous step back. Morrissey must have noticed the increased tension in the air, because he glanced at them in the middle of his work, then laughed, hauling the ladder onto his shoulder and walking down the alley to the back garden again.

"I'm a black belt in judo," he told them. "Haven't done it for a good few years but...you never lose it. Still comes in handy occasionally."

Peyton and Jackson scuttled after him once more, following him to the back and watching as he dumped the ladder down into the shed.

"Did you call the police?" Peyton asked.

"Nah," Morrissey shook his head as he stepped out the shed and closed up the door. He snapped the lock into place and brushed his hands down on his jeans. "I don't really like the police. Prefer to sort things out without them."

Once again, Jackson and Peyton exchanged a quick glance. Did that mean he was the murderer? It certainly meant he was involved in criminal activity to some extent, surely.

"Anyway," Morrissey continued. "You uh...said on the phone you wanted to ask me some questions or something?"

"That's right," said Peyton, trying to keep himself calm in the face of their new and exciting suspect. "Some questions."

"About anything in particular? You guys want to come inside for a cup of tea?"

"Yes please," Jackson eagerly responded, his eyes lighting up at the very mention of tea. "Do you have any biscuits?"

"Think I've got a few digestives," he muttered, leading them in through the back door, which was still unlocked.

"So, you're a...window cleaner," Peyton began, having a little glance round Alan Morrissey's home as he led them through the living room that overlooked the garden and towards the kitchen where he waved his hand to invite them to sit down at the dining room table whilst he made the tea.

"That's right."

"How long have you been doing that?"

"Good few years now."

"I used to be a window cleaner," said Jackson. "Well, a window cleaner's assistant, more like."

"Now he's a detective's assistant," Peyton added brightly. "Are you married at all, Mr Morrissey?"

"Bit of a personal question," Morrissey answered gruffly. "But no. I'm single. Split up with the missus three years back. I prefer being on my own now."

"Thank you, Mr Morrissey," Peyton said politely, glancing at Jackson to see whether he was writing any of this down. Having seen the look and interpreted its meaning, the young lad took out his little note book surreptitiously and held it in the palm of his left hand as he manoeuvred the pen with his right. "You do the houses on Ruskin Road, do you not?"

"They're on my rounds, yeah," confirmed Morrissey with a nod, picking up the now boiled kettle and pouring out the hot water into the three mugs.

"So, you know the Tates, then? Ainsley and his son Gordon?"

"Well, I don't particularly talk to people when I'm cleaning the windows, Mr Kimble. I just knock on the door for my money afterwards. I don't know names."

"Do you know a Mr Lawcock, who lives next door? You gave him your business card. That's how we got your name and number."

"I'm sorry," Morrissey shook his head and placed the cups of tea down on the table, along with a small jug of milk and a bowl of sugar so they could help themselves. Jackson eagerly did so, putting his pad and paper down. "I give everyone my card when I first go round touting for business, and I do a load of different streets in this area...I can't remember everyone."

"Of course," Peyton said understandably. Really, it was too much to expect, and he did believe the man. He probably saw dozens of people on his rounds. He picked up the spoon and
136

dropped a heap of sugar into his tea. "The reason I'm asking, is that young Gordon Tate who lives on that road was murdered last night, and we're investigating his death."

"Really? Wow. Murdered. Seems like a nice area. But what does that have to do with me?" The question had a slight edge to it, as if Morrissey was already becoming impatient with the interrogation, despite his pleasant and polite exterior of inviting them in for tea.

"You were cleaning in that area yesterday, were you not?" asked Peyton.

"Early in the morning, yeah. It was the first place I went on my rounds."

"Did you see anything suspicious?"

"Nope. It was just an ordinary day. I did the windows, collected the money from the people who were in, left cards for the people who weren't to let them know I'd come back some other time, and then moved on to go to the next street along."

"It's just that we noticed the imprints of your ladder, Mr Morrissey," Jackson spoke up, obsessively stirring his tea around and around with the spoon. "Underneath the windows."

"Well, I should imagine so. It had rained the night before and the ground was soft."

"Except the imprints underneath Gordon Tate's window were much deeper than the ones underneath the neighbour's window, Mr Lawcock," said Peyton.

"So?" Morrissey was getting defensive. "I don't know what you're trying to suggest. That I climbed up and killed the guy?"

"You tell me."

137

"Well look, I was there in the morning, and you say the guy was killed during the night. I've got at least a dozen people who can confirm I was there in the morning, including probably that Mr Lawcock guy of yours."

"You could have come back later," Jackson pointed out.

"What motive do I have? I don't even know the kid, for God's sake. This is ridiculous." He stood up now, as if he'd had quite enough with the whole thing. "I think you two should leave."

"But I haven't finished my tea yet," Jackson protested in a childish whine. "And you never gave us those biscuits you promised."

Alan Morrissey looked even more enraged at Jackson's cheekiness, and Peyton quickly decided he needed to calm the situation down before one of them ended up with their arms broken like the burglars. They had broken into the man's shed, after all, although thankfully he was unaware of that.

"Could someone have stolen one of your ladders and used it?" he asked. "Or have you lent a ladder to anyone in the past couple of months?"

The series of questions apparently gave Morrissey pause for thought, and the anger dropped from his features as he stepped back and frowned, looking off to the side for a moment.

"I sold a ladder to a mate of mine about a month ago," he said, taking out a pouch of rolling tobacco from his pocket and opening it up on the table to make himself a cigarette. As he did so, Peyton got the distinct whiff of marijuana coming from the packet. Perhaps that was the reason the man didn't want the police hanging around.

"Now, that's interesting," said Peyton, nodding at Jackson to take up the pen again. The lad put down his cup of tea and did so. "What was his name?"

"Rivers. Timmy Rivers."

Jackson scribbled down the name.

"Do you know anything else about him?" Peyton asked. "Where he lives? Where he works?"

"He works at this uh...factory," Morrissey said. "I only know it cause that's where I dropped off the ladder when I sold it. Helped him load it onto the top of his van when he'd finished work. It was a car place. Royston's."

Peyton's eyes lit up. "That was where Gordon Tate worked. And where I used to work, incidentally."

"Well then, I suppose that makes sense," answered Morrissey. "Although I really don't think Timmy Rivers is your murderer. He's a decent bloke. Maybe someone else there nicked the ladders off him to do the job."

"But it would have to be someone who knew you were doing your rounds in the area that day, so they could time it perfectly and nobody would be suspicious about ladder prints. How well do you know this Timmy Rivers?" asked Peyton. "How can you be so sure that he doesn't have some involvement?"

"Uh...we can never be a hundred per cent sure of anyone, I suppose," said Alan Morrissey with a sigh, sparking up his now rolled cigarette and having a drag. He turned to the cupboards and opened a couple of them up, managing to locate the biscuit tin as promised and offering it out to the pair of them. Jackson dug his hand into the tin immediately and took two out.

"Thanks a lot for your help, Mr Morrissey," said Peyton genuinely.

"Ah, not a problem," Morrissey shrugged.

He was starting to believe the man now. He didn't think that he was involved in the murder and he was probably quite correct when he said he had a dozen or so people who could confirm his alibi. It also seemed too coincidental that he had sold his ladder to someone who worked at the same factory as Gordon Tate. They had planned to go and interview his friends and colleagues at the factory anyway, but now it seemed an even more crucial next step and Peyton was already knocking back his tea quite quickly in his eagerness to get out. Jackson, of course, was savouring his biscuits, dipping them into the tea and sucking on them noisily.

"I'm sorry we accused you of being involved," Peyton added. "But you can understand what it looked like from our point of view."

"Mm, yeah, s'pose so." The window cleaner took a long drag on his cigarette, blew the thick smoke out into the air, then picked up his tea.

Peyton looked over at Jackson to see whether he was almost finished, and made eye contact, silently encouraging him to hurry up. He felt slightly awkward now, as if he didn't know what to say to the man next, and he was glad when they finally did get out of the house a few minutes later, armed with their new information and bundling excitedly into the car again. With all evidence apparently pointing to the factory, it was to Royston's that they went next, determined to find out the truth.

CHAPTER 19

SAM ROYSTON was a nice guy. Peyton had always got on well with him and even viewed him as a bit of a father figure when he'd first joined the workforce at the tender age of eighteen. Now at the age of forty two, Sam was sixty eight and getting ready to retire. He'd had high hopes for Peyton originally, but Peyton had never had the heart to dedicate his entire world to the car industry. For him, it was simply a job that paid the bills and allowed him to get on with his life. It wasn't his passion, unlike how it had been with young Gordon. The lad seemed to flourish in the environment. He loved cars and was always talking about them and it seemed that he and Sam shared the enthusiasm for the work. Peyton was pleased that the boss had found a potential to take over, especially as Sam had no kids of his own. He was married, but his wife had never wanted them apparently, even though he had.

Sam was a great boss, all in all. He always had a friendly smile and a pat on the back for everybody; easy to get along with at all times, and he'd been extremely apologetic and distraught when he'd been forced to let quite a few people go due to the sudden dip in the economy. Peyton wasn't surprised that he was one of the ones who'd lost his job. He'd worked there for years, and it made sense to keep on the fresh blood, the young enthusiastic ones rather than the older, more cynical workers. He didn't resent him for it in the slightest and so, was rather pleased to be popping into the factory that afternoon to speak with him, even if it was under sad circumstances. Despite it only being a couple of months, it already felt like years since he had been there, and he cheerfully said hello to a few of the workers he recognised as they walked across the factory floor to get to the office at the back. They weren't even sure if Timmy Rivers was working that day, and therefore the easiest thing to do would be to ask the boss. Peyton had never heard of this guy, Rivers, but then, he didn't know everyone who worked there by name – not by a long shot.

"Peyton Kimble," Sam cried quite cheerfully as he stood up from his desk to greet them both. "Wasn't expecting to see you here today." The pair clasped hands and shook quite heartily.

"Ah, well – " But Peyton apparently couldn't get a word in edgeways.

"Sit down, sit down..." The boss interrupted, waving his hand towards the two seats already situated opposite his desk then retaking his own seat again and tapping a few keys on his computer with a flourish. "What can I do for the two of you?"

The detective and his assistant took the chairs as requested and sat down, with Peyton rolling his shoulders and preparing for a potentially awkward conversation. Sam seemed quite cheerful and happy, so he was unsure whether he had even heard of Gordon Tate's death or not, and he wasn't particularly looking forward to being the first person to break it to him if he hadn't.

"It's uh...well..." he began hesitantly. "I wish I could come here in better circumstances, Sam, but...it's about Gordon..."

"Oh God, I know," Sam's smile instantly dropped from his face and he adopted a more horrified, shaken expression. He

142

stared down at the desk and shook his head. "Heard about it this morning. Terrible...tragic news...poor lad. I didn't even know he was depressed."

"I know," Peyton agreed with a sigh. "It's very sad and...I know you valued him as part of the company. I'm sorry for your loss."

"He was like a son to me. I mean, I know he had his own father but...I never had my own son. He was like mine...like you were when you were a lad, Peyt. I still have an affection for you, y'know."

Peyton blushed a bit at that. He still respected and looked up to Sam, although he'd never felt particularly jealous or pushed out when Sam started showering his attentions on Gordon instead of him. By that time he was in his late thirties and had long since given up any ambitions of taking over the business, not that he had any in the first place, and he was sure Sam had sensed that. It had been the natural thing for both of them, for him to switch his attention to Gordon, and it had been quite a relief for Peyton not to feel any kind of pressure to deliver.

"I know he was, Sam, and he seemed like a nice guy from what I knew of him. I only spoke to him a few times but...he seemed nice."

"He was. Always making people smile, y'know. He had a lot of friends here, he'll be missed."

"The thing is, er...Sam," Peyton continued, still slightly hesitant considering what he had to tell him next. "The reason we're here to talk to you about Gordon is, I'm not sure if you know this but since I got let go here at the factory I opened up my own detective agency – "

"Oh yes, I read about it in the paper," Sam chuckled. "Kimble Detective Agency. You found some old lady's cat."

"It had been kidnapped, actually," said Peyton, not particularly appreciating the cavalier manner in which Sam was referring to their first case, as if it was just an easy matter of 'finding' the cat. "There was a standoff with an armed kidnapper, a well-known drug dealer who was then arrested. Anyway, the long and the short of it is, we've been employed by Ainsley Tate to investigate his son's death. The police believe it was suicide – "

"Well it was," Sam interrupted. "He left a note."

"Regardless of that, Mr Tate, and indeed the two of us, believe that Gordon was murdered, and we're looking for a suspect in relation to the case, whom we believe might be working here at the factory."

"Murdered?!" cried Sam, then burst out laughing, his fat little chest heaving up and down before he broke out into a coughing fit. He smoked too much and it was beginning to show. He grabbed a handkerchief from the desk and used it to cover up his mouth, raising a hand in the air to show his apology for the outburst. "Sorry...sorry," he mumbled in between taking gasps of air to calm himself down. Once he had regained control of his own breathing and managed to stop both the laughing and the coughing, he looked at them again with an expression of disbelief and repeated the word. "Murdered?"

"We believe so, yes," said Peyton, deadly serious.

"Does a man named Timmy Rivers work here?" asked Jackson, speaking up for the first time since they'd entered the office.

144

"Sorry, who are you?" Sam asked, scrutinising Jackson with a scrunched up nose.

That was when they realised that they hadn't even bothered with introductions. They'd just sat right down and got to business.

"Oh, sorry, this is my partner Jackson Chadwick," Peyton introduced him.

"Doesn't look old enough to be your partner," muttered Sam, some of his initial friendliness gone from his voice in light of the new information and theory Peyton was proffering to him.

"He's a good lad," Peyton insisted. "Knows what he's doing and has proved himself on more than one occasion. Timmy Rivers?" He asked after the name again.

"He works here, yeah."

"Is he in today?"

"Yeah, I think so. I hope so, I mean, he's due to come in."

"We need to speak with him," said Peyton. "Could you take us to where he usually works?" It was more of a command than a request, and where Peyton would normally be subordinate to Sam Royston and do as he was told, now, things were different. Now, they were equals, and perhaps even slightly more than that. Peyton was the superior in the situation; the one running this case and calling the shots, and perhaps Sam Royston knew better than to try and stand in the way of their investigation.

CHAPTER 20

THEIR SUSPICIONS were instantly aroused by the behaviour of young Timmy Rivers. He was in his early twenties, and a good few years younger than the window cleaner Alan Morrissey. Peyton originally found it odd that he and Timmy should be so called friends with one of them being so much older, until he remembered the large age difference between Jackson and himself, and realised he couldn't exactly hold that against the lad.

In the end, it was his shifty eyes and nervous disposition that most alerted his senses, and he immediately felt like Timmy was hiding something and didn't want to talk to them.

"I didn't know Gordon all that well," was one of the first things he said once they mentioned why they were there.

"That's OK, Mr Rivers," said Peyton, being polite and using surnames and prefixes. "We actually want to ask you a couple of questions about someone else you might know, a man named Alan Morrissey."

"Yeah, I know Alan," Timmy answered, glancing back over his shoulder to where Sam Royston was departing to his office having left them alone to talk.

"He sold you a ladder about a month ago, isn't that right?"

"Yeah, what about it?"

"When was the last time you used the ladder, Mr Rivers?"

"I dunno. What's that got to do with anything?"

"Was Gordon a popular guy around here then?" Peyton asked, changing the subject for a moment. "Did he have a lot of friends?"

"I already said, I didn't really know him. I can't talk to you...I've gotta go," he said in a huff, the panic clearly rising in his voice as his wild eyes darted left and right and all around the factory. Then he turned and set off running, abandoning his work and leaving the two of them stood there wondering exactly what it was he had to hide.

"I think we need to find out a bit more about this Timmy Rivers," said Peyton.

"I think you're right, Kimble," agreed Jackson.

There was only so much they could find out on their own, and after a fruitless internet search and another half an hour spent wandering round the factory asking people questions about Gordon only to be told that he was a "nice guy" and "never had any enemies", the pair decided to turn to their contact in the police force – Arthur.

No doubt he was reticent to hear from them again, but if he was, he managed to hide it well. In truth, Peyton hoped he was beginning to get used to the idea of working together, and that they would have a long future ahead helping one another out in investigations.

"Had the results back from the lab," he told them.

"Oh yeah?"

"Yeah. Gordon OD'd on Oxycontin. It's a prescription painkiller."

"Where did he get it? His father said nothing was missing from the medicine cabinet."

"I don't know, but I've heard of some young people crushing it up and using it to try and get high, and seeing as we know he was into drugs anyway, it seems likely he could have got hold of it from one of his friends. How did your interview with Connor Whitley go?"

"Yeah, he was the one who sold him the weed, as we thought," Peyton answered.

"Could he have sold him the other drugs as well?"

"It's possible. Always worth an ask, I suppose."

It didn't fit in with their theory of it being a non-accidental death, however, and Peyton realised that he and Jackson had to continue believing that someone had given Gordon this drug on purpose, knowing that he would overdose on it and, presumably, knowing exactly the right amount to give him.

"So, whoever did this would need a basic knowledge of drugs," Peyton said once they had gotten off the phone.

"Not necessarily," said Jackson. "They could have just done some research; looked it up on the internet. And they obviously used something that gets prescribed to people sometimes, so that it was easily obtainable and not too obviously a murder."

"Well yeah, he's hardly going to use cyanide or some kind of poison, is he? Whoever did this wants to make it look like a suicide, and has gone out of their way to do so."

"They just didn't account for the ladder imprints."

"Well, they did, they just didn't account for the deeper imprints beneath the window, nor the fact that anyone would notice."

"So, it had to be someone who knew the window cleaner was going to be there that day."

"Someone like Timmy Rivers, perhaps," said Peyton, tossing the phone from one hand to the other as they waited for

149

Arthur to call them back. They had requested a background check on the young man at the factory and had requested it speedily performed. Now all they had to do was wait. Arthur was cooperating quite happily, which was a good sign, and things were moving steadily.

"I wonder how they got the drugs into his system though," Jackson speculated. "I mean, if he didn't actually want to die, then surely he would have struggled? That was one of the points why the police didn't think it was murder, right? Because there were no signs of a struggle."

"Unless he was given it whilst he was asleep."

The ring of the phone interrupted their theories and speculation. It was Arthur, getting back to them about Timmy Rivers.

"Couple of previous convictions for fighting, drunk and disorderly. From what I can gather, he's now cleaned up his act and has a full time job in the factory as well as a part time job at weekends working as a window cleaner's apprentice."

With the call on speaker phone, both Jackson and Peyton heard what Arthur had to say, and made eye contact over the news that Rivers was training to be a window cleaner.

"Do you know who he's working for? Who's he an apprentice for?" Peyton asked eagerly.

"I don't know, sorry."

"Do you think it's Alan Morrissey?" asked Jackson quietly.

"No," said Peyton. "He said they were just friends. He would have mentioned if Timmy was his apprentice. It doesn't seem like they know each other all that well. More like just casual acquaintances."

"Who's Alan Morrissey?" asked Arthur, still on the other end of the phone.

"Nobody important," answered Peyton. "One of our early suspects but we've pretty much ruled him out now. Anything else you can tell us about Timmy Rivers? Do you have his address?"

"Er yeah, I can give you that," said Arthur. "It's 47 Booth Street."

"Perfect, thank you, Arthur. I owe you another pint."

"Yes, you do. That's two now."

Peyton grinned and hung up, starting up the engine.

"We heading there next?" Jackson asked.

"Might as well. Seeing as Rivers ran off when we questioned him, it's safe to assume he's probably gone home."

They were still sat outside the factory in their parked up car, having done all they felt they reasonably could do inside. The majority of people were still in there hard at work, with the day not having come to an end yet, although they'd seen a couple of guys nip out for a fag break in the time they'd been on the phone.

Now though, their attention was attracted by Sam Royston himself, emerging from the staff back door of the factory with his phone in his hand. He was staring at it with a concerned expression on his face and seemed distracted, anxious. He pressed a few buttons and then pressed the phone to his ear, pacing up and down, back and forth as he spoke to someone on the other end, at one point becoming quite animated and angry, waving his hand around but, at the same time, apparently trying to be quiet, glancing over his shoulder towards the door and keeping his voice low.

Jackson even rolled down the window casually so that they might attempt to overhear what he was talking about as the two of them watched him in interested silence, but all they could hear was his hushed voice, as though he was speaking in a stage whisper.

Then, just as quickly as it had begun, the call ended, and Sam was stalking over towards his car, taking out the keys and blipping the alarm off.

"What was all that about?" Jackson asked.

"God knows," Peyton replied with a shrug, releasing the handbrake and rolling the car away to the right and out the car park, their entertainment for the afternoon now over and their new plan to go to Timmy Rivers' house and find out what he had to hide.

CHAPTER 21

IT WAS JACKSON who noticed the other car first.

Peyton was concentrating too much on his driving, trying to follow the directions of the annoying woman on the Sat Nav who kept telling him to turn 'sharp left' right at the last minute, and then helpfully informing him that they were going the wrong way. It was a good job he hadn't been a taxi driver. He had a fairly terrible sense of direction unless he had a decent map to help him. The Sat Nav was good the majority of the time, but the woman was having an off day, it would appear.

"I think we might be getting followed," Jackson said quietly, turning round to look out the back window at the car that was driving directly behind them.

"What?! What do you mean? What makes you say that?"

"Well, this car has been behind us for like...pretty much the entire way."

"Even when we turned down the wrong road?" asked Peyton in a bit of a panic.

"No, not then. It stayed on the main road, but when we re-joined it again, the car ended up behind us after those traffic lights."

"Oh. Could be a coincidence then."

"Could be," agreed Jackson. "I'm just being cautious."

"Well, that's good, Chadwick. It's good to be cautious." He glanced in the rear view mirror at the car behind, then frowned. "Hang on a minute. I think that's...I think that's Sam."

"Sam?"

"Sam Royston."

"Seriously?" Jackson twisted round again and squinted hard at the car.

"Well don't be so obvious about it," Peyton chastised him, putting his hand on Jackson's shoulder and trying to turn him back round.

"Why would Sam Royston be following us?"

"I don't know. But he went to his car, didn't he? We were already in our car and then he went to his car, so it makes sense that he'd be behind us."

"Going in exactly the same direction for the past twenty minutes?"

"Does seem a bit...odd," Peyton admitted, checking the mirror again. Sure enough, the car was still there. Now it was beginning to concern him. "He didn't see us though, did he? He didn't see us watching him when he was on the phone?"

"I don't know," said Jackson. "I don't think so. Can't be certain."

They drove on in silence for a little while longer.

"What shall we do?" Jackson asked eventually.

"I don't know," Peyton admitted. "I suppose we should...try and lose him. Or...try to find out if he really is following us. That's what people do in films, isn't it?"

"Yeah. They make a sudden turn on purpose or something, or pull up for a moment and stop the car. Then if the person isn't actually following them they'll just go right on past."

"OK yes, let's do that then."

Their plan agreed, Peyton took a sudden left turn onto a quieter street and parked up their car for a moment, waiting.

Jackson twisted round in his seat and looked out the back window, just in time to see the red car that had been trailing them sail on past and go straight through the green traffic lights on the main road. He breathed a sigh of relief, his shoulder sagging as he turned back round with a smile on his face.

"He's gone."

"Excellent," cried Peyton, moving off the kerb and doing a three point turn to get them back towards the main road. "So, he wasn't following us after all. Just a coincidence that we happened to be heading in the same direction."

"Yeah," agreed Jackson, nodding. "Yeah, just a coincidence. Thank God for that. Thought I was in some spy movie for a minute there."

"Yeah, me too," laughed Peyton, turning left again and getting back on the right track before the Sat Nav woman began shouting at them. He popped the radio on quietly in the background for the remainder of their journey. They only had another five minutes to go to their destination and the majority of it passed without incident, until Peyton noticed something else to put them both on alert.

"Isn't that Sam's car again?" he asked, pointing directly in front of them.

"Uh...yeah...think so..."

That in itself, wasn't so unusual. They had allowed the car to pass them and now it was in front; nothing odd about that. The strange part, was what happened next.

The car took a right. So did they.

The car took a left. So did they.

The roles had been reversed. Now, it was no longer Sam who was following them, but them who were following Sam.

"Prepare to arrive at destination in 400 yards," the mechanical American voice of the Sat Nav spoke to them.

Sam's car was pulling up ahead of them. About 400 yards ahead of them.

"He's coming here too," Peyton spoke what they were both thinking. "He wasn't following us..."

"And we weren't following him..."

"We were just both going to the same place."

"Timmy Rivers' house."

"Pull up here," said Jackson, reaching over and literally taking the wheel. "Don't let him see us."

"Alright, alright!" Peyton swerved a bit, then went up onto the kerb, silencing the engine by turning the key in the ignition. Jackson was quite right though. It wouldn't do to make Sam aware of all their skulking around. "He probably thinks *we* followed *him.*"

"He probably hasn't even noticed. Most people don't."

"Eh...you're right, I suppose."

They fell silent as they watched Sam Royston get out of his car, lock it up, and wander up the path to Timmy Rivers' house. It was a nice residential street. Old council build now owned by the residents. Peyton imagined that Timmy probably lived there with his parents. He didn't seem old enough to be able to afford to get on the property ladder.

"Well, we can't go and speak to him now," sighed Peyton.

"At least we know he's in. That must have been who Sam was speaking to on the phone."

"We'll just have to wait till he comes out." He drummed his fingers against the edge of the steering wheel impatiently.

156

"I wonder what he's here for anyway."

"God knows. He seemed quite...upset on the phone."

"He did."

They lapsed into silence again, then Jackson spoke up.

"We should go over there."

"Over where?"

"To the house."

Peyton turned and gave him an odd look. "But they'll see us."

"We can be sneaky."

"Are you suggesting we creep up and spy on them?"

Jackson hesitated. "Er...well...uh...yes? I suppose."

Peyton considered it for a moment, but it was only a brief moment, because in reality he had been just as much an adventurous child as Jackson was, and he couldn't resist the idea once it was put forward. "Alright then," he agreed casually, as if he was agreeing to having chips for tea. Then he was opening up the car door and getting out, trying to be as silent as possible about it despite his haste to run over and see what was going on.

Jackson looked at Peyton in amazement, not quite believing that he'd agreed to this so readily, then he wasted no more time in leaping out the passenger side and joining him. They quietly closed the car doors and locked up using the key in the keyhole rather than pressing the button and causing the alarm to make that loud blipping sound. They didn't want to alert anyone to their presence.

Then, side by side, they very slowly walked – crept – the remaining few metres from their car to Sam Royston's car, which was parked directly outside Timmy Rivers' house.

Peyton took the lead at that point, putting his arm out and flattening his hand against Jackson's chest to push him back a bit, the two of them hiding behind the tall hedge that lined the wall at the bottom of the Rivers' front garden. Definitely his parents' house, Peyton thought to himself again. He didn't look like the type to keep his garden looking so nice.

Using the overgrown hedges as cover, they edged up bit by bit, their feet shuffling across the pavement, then Peyton leaned out and peered round the corner.

From there, he could see that the front door was open, not all the way, just slightly ajar, and in the immediate window on the right hand side of the door, he could see two figures stood in what he imagined was the living room of the house, talking to one another in an animated fashion.

"I think they're having an argument," he hissed back at Jackson, who was currently unable to see due to his position just behind Peyton.

"Can you hear anything?"

"Not really. Can you?"

"No. Let's go closer." Jackson nudged him in the shoulder, urging him onwards.

Peyton grimaced and assessed the situation. It was quite a risk. If the two of them just ran into the garden, there was a very good chance that both men inside would spot them. Then again, they seemed quite distracted and caught up in their own conversation. He looked around for a potential spot deeper in the front garden where they could hide. Perhaps they could go and situate themselves directly beneath the living room window, but that was fairly exposed and when Sam came out he would definitely see them sat there.

The only other option, then, was the row of bushes that separated the Rivers' garden from their neighbour's on the left. They looked fairly prickly and probably uncomfortable to hide in, but hopefully it wouldn't be for long and he was sure they'd be able to hear what was going on due to their close proximity to the open door.

Then, as he looked over to the window again, he realised the two men had moved away from it and deeper into the house. He could still see their shadows somewhere in there, but they weren't as close as they'd been previously, and Peyton took this as a sign to seize the moment and take their opportunity to make a move.

"Now!" he said in a loud whisper, grabbing Jackson by the sleeve of his coat and tugging him outwards into the front garden. He half crouched down like he'd seen people do in films, and kept his head low as he raced towards the bushes on the left hand side of the door.

He held his arms up to protect his face as he broached them, pushing back the brambles and forcing his way in, making quite a loud rustling sound which he was almost certain would attract attention and he was immediately marking this down as a bad idea. Another bad ideas – like breaking into the garden shed.

Jackson was close behind him and pushed his way in too, the pair of them twisting round to face the front and settling themselves down on their backsides in the earthy ground inside the bush. They were barely shielded by the autumn brambles, the majority of the small green leaves now turned to brown and dropping off; and the branches that had once housed them rudely sticking into their arms and their faces as a punishment for invading nature's space. It was, as Peyton had imagined, entirely uncomfortable, and probably not even a very good hiding spot.

Before he'd had chance to settle down and strain his ears to hear what was going on, he realised in a panic that both their feet were still sticking out the front of the bush, to the extent that Sam Royston would probably trip over them if he attempted to walk out the door and go down the garden path in the next minute or so.

"Feet," he hissed to Jackson, the bushes still rustling and the branches crackling as they tried to get comfortable and adjust their positions, cradling their legs tightly against their chest by folding their arms over the top and tucking in their feet even further, till their heels were pressed up against their bottoms. And still the bushes rustled and the branches crackled. "Now be quiet."

"It's not me," Jackson muttered. "It's the bloody bush!"

"Shhh!"

Peyton had the brief thought that he was far too old to be running around doing all this type of stuff, then he almost immediately quashed it from his mind when his ears pricked up and he heard what was going on inside.

"Just stick with what we agreed," Sam was saying, apparently calmer now that they had finished their argument, although he still sounded worked up and stressed.

"I'm just nervous," replied another voice, that of Timmy Rivers, as they'd suspected.

"Well don't be," said Sam. "You'll be fine. Just stick with the story. And remember the money, OK?"

"Yeah," said Timmy.

"And your future. You've got a bright future now, you know that, don't you? It's all yours for the taking. All you have to do is
160

keep your head down, stay cool. You can do that for me, can't you, Timmy? Stay cool."

"Stay cool. Yeah, I can do that, Sam."

"Good lad. I knew I could rely on you."

"That's not what you said earlier."

"Ha!" Sam gave a hearty laugh followed by what sounded like a slap on the back for Timmy. "Come back to work for the last hour. Otherwise people will get suspicious."

"OK, Sam."

"Good lad," Sam said again, his voice getting louder as it got closer. Peyton, peeking through the bushes, could see him in the doorway now, and guessed he was saying his goodbyes to Timmy and was about to walk down the path towards his car.

He nudged Jackson to stay silent, and the two of them sat completely still in their hiding place. Peyton could hardly bear to look. He still felt so utterly exposed despite being half secluded by the bush. He wished he'd worn some camouflage gear instead of his ordinary blue jeans; if only he'd known they'd be doing something like this. He bowed his head against his knees and closed his eyes up tightly.

"See you around, Timmy," said Sam, his voice sounding like it was right next to them. "And remember what I said."

"I will," said Timmy from the doorstep.

There was a crunching of feet along the gravel and the sound of footsteps receding down the garden path. As Peyton dared to look up from his knees once they were finally gone, he turned to Jackson to find his young accomplice was doing exactly the same thing – hiding his face and most probably holding his breath too.

"It's OK," he whispered. "I think he's gone."

161

A moment later and they heard the sound of a car starting and tyres scraping along the road as it drove away. Then the front door closed shut and they were left alone in the deathly silence that followed, cramped up in the bushes and quietly reflecting on what they had heard. They needed to discuss it, and soon.

Sticking his head out from the brambles, Peyton looked over at the window to check no one was looking, then scrambled out into the garden again, rolling over onto his shoulder and ungracefully landing flat on his back before springing up to his feet and dashing down the path and out round the corner to where they were standing before, wanting to be fairly quick and not risk the chance of Timmy Rivers seeing them.

Jackson followed suit, and soon they were both back where they started and walking towards the car as they picked bits of twigs and leaves off of their clothes.

"I'm calling a meeting," Peyton announced, hurrying to the car and unlocking it. He opened up the door and slipped into the driver's seat whilst Jackson ran round the other side and got in next to him.

"Did you hear what he said?" Jackson asked, his eyes wide.

"I did."

"Do you think he's involved in all this then? Sam?"

"I don't know," Peyton frowned, then shook his head. "Not Sam. He can't be. He's just not that type of guy."

"How do you know?"

"I've known him all my life. Or most of it, at least."

"Well then, what was he talking about?" Jackson asked pertinently. "You heard what he was saying. Something about money. And sticking to their agreements. Keeping cool.

Remember what we discussed. All that kind of stuff. What does it mean?"

"I don't know, Chadwick. I don't know any more than you do."

"He's up to something though, like we thought. That Timmy. He's hiding something."

"Oh yes, he definitely is. And whatever it is, it does seem like Sam is involved with it somehow too. It's nothing to do with the murder though," said Peyton, quite confident about that. "It's something else entirely, and it's probably shaken them up a bit because there's now a lot of attention on them. Maybe they're....fiddling the books or something over at the factory, and now they're worried about getting caught out. That's why he was talking about money."

"I thought you said he was a nice guy."

"Who? Sam? He is a nice guy."

"Well then why would he be fiddling the books?"

"I don't know," cried Peyton, exasperated.

"What are we going to do?" Jackson asked. "What's the plan now?" He always looked to Peyton whenever plans were needed, and the detective felt the sudden weight of pressure, of expectation. It was difficult always being the leader, being the one that everyone expected to come up with the great ideas.

"Uh...the plan is..." He responded vaguely, desperately searching his mind to think of one. "Well....let's go in and talk to Timmy Rivers as we'd planned. If he does as Sam told him and heads off back to work then we'll end up missing him again and we'll miss our opportunity to speak with him. Besides, he'll probably still be a bit rattled by his conversation with Sam and we might be able to pick something up."

163

"Good idea," Jackson grinned, instantly back on side and back in a positive mood about the whole thing.

A minute later, and the two of them were stood on the doorstep directly next to the place where they'd been hiding out in the bush, and ringing the bell waiting for Timmy to answer.

He took one look at them and instantly tried to close the door in their faces, but Peyton was quick to react and slotted his foot into the space, stopping it from closing and biting down on his lip at the pain the impact actually caused him. It didn't look that painful on the television.

"We just want a quick word with you, Mr Rivers," he told him.

"Well, I've got nothing to say, I already told you."

"I've been speaking to my contact at Cheshire Constabulary Police Force, and he seems to think differently."

The mention of the actual police – rather than a couple of ambling amateurs – seemed to instil the correct kind of response in Rivers. He paled considerably and faltered in his resolve to be rid of them, allowing them to linger on the doorstep. Peyton took that as his cue to continue speaking.

"We know about your previous convictions."

Timmy opened his mouth in protest, as if to say something, but Peyton cut him dead, holding a hand up in the air.

"And we know you don't do that type of thing anymore. Which is wonderful. You've moved on. That's great." He smiled at him enthusiastically.

"Well then why are you bothering me with all these questions?"

"We also know that you work part time on weekends as a window cleaner's apprentice."

164

"Right," Timmy grunted. "What's that got to do with anything?"

"Is that why Alan Morrissey sold you one of his ladders?"

"Yeah, that's right."

"How long have you known Mr Morrissey? He referred to you as a 'friend'."

"I've known him for a few years, yeah. Since I was a kid. He was more of a friend of my Dad's than anything, but after my Dad died me and him became pretty close. He's a decent guy. Looks after me."

"Gave you a good deal on the ladder then, did he?"

"Yeah, he did. What of it?"

"Do you mind me asking, Timmy," said Jackson, scratching his nose and acting as though he was a little confused. "Why do you actually need a ladder?"

"Well, I'm a window cleaner's apprentice. Thought you already knew that."

"But surely, the window cleaner whom you're working for already has ladders. I had a bit of a job doing windows myself not so long ago, and I never needed to bring my own ladder. Seems a bit...excessive."

"Well I do, alright? I need my own ladder. That's all there is to it. Now, if you don't mind...I need to get back to work." And with that, he came outside and pushed in between the two of them, closing the door behind him and walking down the drive.

Jackson and Peyton followed, with Peyton posing a few more questions.

"Do you get on well with Sam then? He's a nice guy, isn't he?"

"Well, you should know. You used to work there, didn't you?"

"Yeah. Do you remember me?"

"Not really. We worked in a different section."

"Yeah, we did. So, you get on well with Sam then?"

Timmy unlocked his car and opened the door. "He's alright, yeah, he's a good boss." He climbed in and went to close the door, but once again, Peyton stopped him.

"And what about the guy you work for on the weekends? Your window cleaning boss? What's he like?"

"Decent, yeah."

"What's his name?"

"Ed."

"Ed what?"

"Ed Norfolk." He forced the door and Peyton jerked his hand back just in time as it slammed to a close.

"Are you working tomorrow, Mr Rivers?" He shouted through the window.

The young man ignored him, revved the engine, and took off, speeding down the street and turning at the end of the road.

"Well," Jackson said once he was gone. "I think we rattled him a bit."

"I think we did," Peyton agreed with a chuckle. "Good job, Chadwick."

"Ah, you weren't so bad yourself, Kimble. What now?"

Peyton glanced at his watch, considering their options. "Try and find out more about this Ed Norfolk that he works for. See if he's on police record maybe."

"Uncle Arthur again then? You really are gonna have to take him for a pint, y'know."

"I'll do it tonight," Peyton suddenly decided, a crafty plan forming. "That's how I'll win him round. Pints after work. Three of them. He can bring the results to the pub with him and we can discuss the case."

"Do you want me there too then?"

"No, Chadwick. You go home and be with your mother. She might be a little shaken up after today and she will have spent the majority of it comforting Ainsley Tate. Remember that he's still on our list of suspects and will have to stay there until we've managed to eliminate him entirely or until someone else has taken his place. Find out what you can about him, about how he's been reacting to his son's death, the type of things he's been saying, how they've spent the day."

"You want me to interrogate my own mother about her boyfriend?"

"Ish. Do the best you can without making it obvious."

"Speaking of our list of suspects," said Jackson, getting out his notepad as they walked back to their own car. "We haven't added to it for a while. It still says Ainsley Tate and Alan Morrissey. Want me to cross Morrissey off now?"

Peyton sighed, then slowly shook his head. "No, leave him on for the time being, but perhaps we should put stars next to the people we believe are more suspicious."

"Who are we giving stars to then?"

"Write down Timmy Rivers, and give him a star."

"It's like being at school," Jackson cracked a joke, scribbling down the name and then a little pentagonal star next to it. "What about Sam Royston? I know you like him, Kimble, but you have to admit they were talking about something....dodgy. He should at least get his name down, even if he's only a minor suspect."

"Alright. Put his name down, but I'm sure there's a reasonable explanation for their rather odd conversation."

"And argument," Jackson pointed out, his impartial stance proving to have the better memory.

"Yeah. Yeah, OK, put him down."

"I already have done. And that Ed Norfolk too. Might as well. It's quite a list we've got now, Kimble."

"We're narrowing them down though, Chadwick. Timmy Rivers is still our main suspect, and after tonight, we'll hopefully know a bit more about this Norfolk chap."

CHAPTER 22

THE PUB WAS LIVELY and cheerful already by the time Peyton arrived. It was a Friday night, he supposed, and people were getting off work early and coming to have a good old drink with their mates. He'd opted for the Wetherspoons again. It was cheap enough to be able to afford to buy Arthur drinks, and the food was decent. He'd ordered himself a plate of nachos as a sort of starter, as he'd promised Sherri he'd eat with her later. He felt like it had been ages since they'd sat down and enjoyed one another's company – he'd been so caught up in his cases since it all started.

Arthur arrived five minutes after he did and found Peyton sat in the same corner spot with the two pints on the table already waiting for him. He smiled at his younger brother and sat down, flattening his briefcase out on the seat next to him and picking up his drink to have a couple of sips of the cool, refreshing liquid.

"How are you?" he asked Peyton. "How've you been getting on?"

"Had a productive afternoon," Peyton flashed him a quick smile back and then filled him in on what they'd been doing – including the little trip to the factory, their run in with Timmy Rivers and the way they'd gone back to his house to speak with him further and ended up overhearing a strange argument between him and Sam Royston.

"Hmm, that is odd," Arthur admitted. "Can't imagine Sam being mixed up in anything too bad though. He's a decent bloke is Sam."

"Yeah, he is," Peyton agreed. "Anyway, how did you get on with that name I gave you?" He was anxious to hear the results, the real reason why he was plying his brother with alcohol yet again.

"You mean your man Ed Norfolk? Nothing," Arthur shook his head apologetically. "He hasn't got a record so there's nothing on file for him. I tried full names too. Edward. Eddie. Nope. The guy's clean. Then I did a basic internet search for him, driver's licence search, stuff like that. Also nothing."

"He doesn't have a driver's licence?"

"Not under that name at least. By that point, it had sort of got my attention. So I did some more digging around. Couldn't find a birth certificate, bank account, national insurance number, mortgage, anything...couldn't find a single thing for Ed Norfolk."

Peyton frowned, staring across the table at Arthur in confusion. "So...what are you...what are you trying to say? That...this guy doesn't exist?"

"I don't think he does, no. I think he's a ghost. You're chasing a ghost. Which, as far as I'm concerned, puts a load more suspicion on your man Timmy Rivers."

"He made it up? He made up this...Ed Norfolk?"

"It would seem that way, yeah."

"As some sort of cover?"

"Possibly. I don't know. You're into this deeper than I am."

Peyton took a sip of his pint. "That's amazing."

"Pretty interesting, isn't it?" Arthur had to admit with a chuckle.

"What should I do?"

"I don't know, Peyt. I thought you were the master detective now."

"What would you do though, Arty? I mean, hypothetically speaking...if this was your case, your responsibility...what would you do?"

"Hypothetically speaking....uh....I would probably trail the guy. If he's claiming to be working as window cleaner's apprentice for this Ed Norfolk but he's actually not, then I'd want to know what he was really doing on weekends."

Peyton pursed his lips as he pondered the idea, then slowly nodded. "How did you find out he was doing this window thing in the first place?" he asked. "It was on his record?"

"Yeah, he'd obviously told his social worker that, and his social worker had put it on his latest report, just to prove that he was doing well and didn't need any more close monitoring etc."

"How long ago was that then?"

"About a month."

"Roundabout the time Alan Morrissey sold him the ladder."

"That your other window cleaning bloke?" Arthur asked.

"Yeah."

"I'd keep your eye on him too then. Find out what he does at the weekends, whether the two of them meet up."

"Yeah. Good idea. Thanks Arthur." Peyton smiled and clinked his glass against his brother's.

"Yeah, yeah, OK. Just don't tell anyone I'm helping you, will you? I'll never hear the end of it."

As promised, Peyton spent the remainder of that evening at home with his wife Sherri. He'd been working so hard that he hadn't had enough time recently to devote to her and it felt nice to be able to catch up and relax. They had a pleasant meal together and a curl up on the sofa watching television. She asked him all about the case and how it was progressing, and he told her most of the details, but not all. He asked after her work and how things were going at the school.

"I might have a case for you after you've finished with this one," she stroked his chest with a smile and nuzzled up against his shoulder, the two of them now sat on the sofa in front of the TV letting their dinner go down.

"Oh yeah?" He raised an eyebrow.

"It's probably too small to go to the official police with but the kids involved are insisting I bring in some sort of private detective, and of course they all know about you now since you became a local hero."

"Well, I wouldn't call it that," Peyton blushed a bit, but asked after the details of the case regardless.

"There's a piece of student art work gone missing, and with the final exams coming up in three weeks' time, the young girl's convinced that someone's stolen it to try and sabotage her grades."

"Why would anyone do that?"

"I don't know. She is one of the more popular girls in the school and expected to achieve high grades. Could be jealousy. She's even named a few suspects, including one girl that she fell out with recently over something petty. She called it boy issues but wouldn't say anything more. All her friends are insisting it's sabotage too."

"She couldn't have just...lost...the artwork?"

172

"That's what I said originally. That it was probably just misplaced somewhere and that I was sure it would turn up, but then she said it was taken from her locked locker. Now, we have CCTV in the locker room area so we checked it and, sure enough, someone came in with a hood on to disguise their features, broke into the locker and stole it."

"Wow," Peyton was impressed by the level of intrigue in the 'Case of the Missing Art Project' as he was already dubbing it inside his own mind. He promised Sherri he and Jackson would look into it as soon as this little adventure was over, and Sherri went on to say that she felt particularly sorry for the girl involved because she was an orphan from a broken home, which led the conversation onto new ground.

"Ainsley Tate's an orphan," Peyton stated.

"Is he? That's interesting. Did you ask him about it?"

"Nah. I don't like to pry. I suppose some people don't like talking about things like that."

"But he told you about it in the first place, opened up to you...maybe he wanted you to ask more questions."

"I don't know," shrugged Peyton. "Do you not mind talking about it?"

"Not at all. It's part of who I am..."

"It made me think of our brother again."

"Ah yes, the long lost missing Kimble," Sherri smiled and kissed his cheek. "You going to start trying to track him down again?"

She had helped him, all those years ago when they'd first started dating and when he was keenly interested in the idea of finding their adopted brother, and had even been quite disappointed when he'd given up.

"Don't think so," he shook his head. "No point is there..."

"Well, you never know, he might be out there looking for *you*."

"Did you ever try and look for your birth parents?"

"I did, yeah. Had about as much luck as you trying to find your brother. Gave up, tried not to think about it again and...well...got on with my life and met you and settled down. I suppose I still think about it occasionally. Wonder if they're still out there, what they're up to...whether they ever regret their decision."

"I know my mum did," Peyton sighed, remembering the many nights afterwards he'd heard her crying in her sleep and occasionally calling out what sounded like the boy's name. But their father had been so insistent on giving him up. It was for the best, he'd said. For the best. What did that even mean? He'd come from a fairly comfortable, middle class family. They weren't particularly struggling, financially. He was sure they could have afforded to bring up another child. So why get rid of it? Again, the questions resurfaced in his mind and once again, he pushed them to the side, suggesting to Sherri that they head up for bed. There was no point thinking of all this now and allowing it to clog up his head, not when he was supposed to be getting to the bottom of this murder. He needed to be fresh and on top of his game the following morning. He intended to set out early and follow Timmy Rivers.

CHAPTER 23

IT WAS A PHONE CALL that awoke Peyton Kimble early the next morning rather than the phone alarm that he'd set to wake him at seven thirty, and he was surprised to see Jackson's name on the caller ID. He hadn't put him down as a morning person and he was wondering what he was doing up so soon.

"Chadwick?" He half yawned into the mouthpiece, sitting up and rubbing his eyes. He glanced over at Sherri. She had stirred and yawned a little but other than that was still asleep.

"Kimble. What's the plan for today then?" he asked, all full of energy, then promptly answered his own question. "I thought we could maybe trail Sam Royston some more. Yesterday we saw him go to the house of one of our suspects and get into an argument with him. I wonder what we'll see him do today."

"Probably very little, considering it's a Saturday," Peyton answered. "Go to the shops maybe. I thought it'd be a much better idea for us to trail Timmy Rivers today," he went on to explain, although he was pleased they both had it in their heads to trail someone. It showed that they were at least thinking along the same lines and being proactive in their suggestions. "He's supposed to be on his window cleaning shift today but after my little meeting with Arty last night, I found out that this Ed Norfolk is a complete fantasy."

"What? How d'you mean?"

"He doesn't exist. Arthur did a bit of work, checked the records for me, and there is no such person as Edward Norfolk or whatever his name is. Timmy Rivers made him up to throw us, and apparently everyone else too, off his scent."

"Why? What's he up to?"

"Exactly, Chadwick!" cried Peyton. "What is he up to indeed? That's exactly what I intend to find out today."

"You're gonna trail him then?"

"I am. I presume you're coming? You are my partner..."

"Well actually, I think I'm going to stick with trailing Sam Royston," Jackson said quietly on the other end of the phone, as if a little nervous about upsetting the man who was effectively his boss. "It's just something that mum said last night..."

"Your mum?"

"Yeah. You know how you asked me to subtly question her about Ainsley Tate?"

"Yes?" Peyton prompted expectantly, eager to hear what new news he had.

"Well, I did it. I don't think he's particularly a suspect anymore, at least...for me he's not. I dunno, I've just got a feeling."

"A feeling?"

"Yeah. I get 'em sometimes. I think I might be psychic."

"Yeah right," scoffed Peyton. "Just get on with it."

"She said he was upset and stuff, as you might expect, but then he said something else, that was a bit interesting. He said that he thought something that had happened at work had upset Gordon, that he came back home one day and was all distracted over something and didn't want to talk...went straight to his room and acted strange..."

"Was that recently?"

"Yeah, like...three days before he died. And you know what Ainsley said about work being Gordon's only social life. He didn't really go out much or anything like that, so it stands to reason that it *must* have been something that happened at work...and after what we saw and heard go down with Sam and Timmy yesterday, I think we need to keep an eye on Sam too."

Peyton considered it for a moment, frowning as he rubbed his still slightly sleepy eyes and stood up off the bed, padding through to the bathroom to start to get himself ready to head out. "Yeah," he eventually said, nodding even though Jackson was on the other end of the phone and wouldn't be able to see him. "Yeah, you're right. I tell you what we'll do then...we'll split up today. You keep an eye on Sam, and I'll keep an eye on Timmy."

"Yeah, that was what I was trying to suggest," Jackson protested with a small chuckle. "Don't try and pretend this was all your idea, Kimble."

"Alright, alright," Peyton grumbled good naturedly. "You're a handy partner, Chadwick. I admit that."

Their phone call done and dusted and their arrangement set up for the remainder of the day, Peyton got a quick wash, dressed himself and headed on out. The two of them had arranged to liaise with one another by mobile and keep in touch about what was going on at their respective stake outs, although Peyton was fairly convinced he was getting the more interesting end of the deal. If Timmy Rivers wasn't window cleaning on a Saturday morning, then what exactly *was* he doing?

Time to find out.

The address was still programmed into Peyton's Sat Nav from the day previously and after quickly kissing Sherri goodbye, he drove over there, arriving by half past eight. He wasn't sure what time Timmy would be leaving to go to his "window cleaning" or whatever it was he was getting up to, but he wanted to ensure he was there in plenty of time and didn't miss him. He wasn't exactly sure how Jackson was planning to tail Sam Royston without having an actual car to utilise, but that wasn't his problem at the current moment as he pulled up outside the familiar house of Timmy Rivers and switched off the engine to his car.

He drummed his fingers on the steering wheel and waited. He was a good metre or so down from the house, but could still clearly see the front door, and wouldn't miss Timmy if he came out to get in the car and drive away, and so he sat there, and waited. And waited. And waited.

The hours seemed to pass by so slowly he felt like he was going insane. The first hour was the longest, then the second went a bit quicker, but the third dragged and dragged. He was watching the clock on his car and counting along every single minute, concentrating so hard on that that a couple of times he thought he'd missed something exciting going on at the house. But no; the car was still there, and the curtains hadn't twitched or moved in the slightest.

The first signs of life came at around 12am. Somebody came down to the living room windows and opened up the curtains. Peyton woke up from his daydream and watched with interest. It was an older woman in her fifties, whom he imagined to be Timmy's mother. She looked tired and was
178

wearing a dressing gown. After opening the curtains, she disappeared and wasn't seen again for another half an hour, when she returned and switched on the television, sitting down to watch it.

By this time, Peyton's stomach was beginning to grumble and he was starting to wish he'd brought lunch. He hadn't actually expected to be there for that long. He had been fully expecting Timmy Rivers to have done something by now, but to all intents and purposes it seemed the young man was still tucked up in bed having a good old fashioned Saturday lie in. Maybe he didn't actually do anything on a Saturday. But then why would he need to lie, set up a whole cover for himself?

None of it made sense.

He began to hope that Jackson was having a little more luck with Sam Royston.

CHAPTER 24

JACKSON DIDN'T HAVE a car.

He hadn't actually passed his test and although he had a provisional licence, he had failed on three occasions. This didn't stop him, however, from stealing his mother's car keys that Saturday morning and taking the motor out for a spin. He didn't tell anyone what he was doing, of course, not even Peyton, and he was glad that the detective didn't ask *how* he would be doing the actual trailing.

As far as he was concerned, he was a fairly decent driver. He'd just had bad luck on the tests and a few nasty roundabouts. He'd just try his best to avoid those when he was out and about that morning, and hopefully the traffic wouldn't be too bad seeing as it was a Saturday and it was bright and early. In fact, that was *why* he'd gotten up so early in the first place; because he wanted to make sure he stole his mother's car before she woke up and realised it was gone or what he was up to. He'd already been out in it and parked up in a layby when he'd rang Peyton. The plan had been in motion long before the conversation with his 'boss' and he'd been fully intending to trail Sam Royston whether he had Peyton's backing or not.

Peyton had a personal connection to Sam. The guy had taken him on when he was a young man, given him a job when he'd failed his exams and given him a chance, then basically ensured him employment throughout the majority of his adult life. It was entirely understandable that Peyton would be reluctant to place any kind of suspicion or blame on the man. Jackson would probably feel the same about Peyton Kimble, if any suspicion were to fall on him some many years into the future. He couldn't imagine it, however, but that was exactly why he felt he was in the best position to look at the entire situation from a non-emotional and logical point of view. He had no personal connection to Sam Royston and felt no loyalty. It made sense that they were doing things this way – that Peyton should be after Timmy whilst Jackson was after Sam.

The first thing he'd had to do the previous evening, however, was get hold of Sam Royston's personal address. He'd figured that he probably wouldn't be at the factory on a Saturday, so he'd simply looked him up online and managed to get a location for him. It hadn't been particularly difficult. Just twenty minutes of internet browsing that anyone could do.

So the next morning he was there, bright and early, sat in his mum's parked up car, and waiting.

He didn't know exactly what was going to happen, if anything. It could be exactly as Peyton had predicted, and that Sam Royston would live his Saturday like any other normal man in Cheshire, or indeed the UK. Get up late, perhaps go to the shops, take his dog for a walk if he had one, laze around and generally not do very much. Maybe he'd go out for a few pints in the evening with his friends, if he had any. Jackson didn't know anything about Sam Royston at all, but when he saw a woman come down to open the curtains in the living room at

182

CARS, CATS & CROOKS

around 9am, he presumed that it was his wife. She looked about the right age to be married to him at least.

He watched for a little while as she turned on the television and flicked through the channels. Then he saw Sam come in, buttoning up his shirt. He kissed her on the cheek then disappeared off again. Five minutes or so later, maybe less, the front door opened and Sam came out.

He was dressed in a shirt and a pair of jeans, a more casual appearance than the suit he wore at work, but he still looked smart and ready to go out for the day. He glanced up and down the street then got into his car.

Jackson slunk down in the seat of his own car and tried his best to not get spotted, feeling completely self-conscious and exposed. As Sam's car pulled off the kerb and passed directly to the left of Jackson's car, he dived down in the seat completely and flattened himself out, hiding from the windows until the sound of the engine had receded into the distance. Then he jerked back up again, hurriedly started up his own engine and whizzed the car round to follow Sam's.

He was a little far ahead, but he caught sight of him in the distance and pressed his foot down on the accelerator to catch up as they passed onto the main road, making sure not to get too close and occasionally allow other cars to get in front of them. As long as he could still see Sam's car ahead of him, that was all that mattered. He wasn't even paying any attention whatsoever to any of the other cars on the road, something that was perhaps inadvisable for an uninsured driver who hadn't passed their test and was currently in their mother's stolen vehicle, but Jackson had never been one to follow rules.

After a while, he started to feel quite relaxed about the whole thing, and found that devoting all his attention and concentration to Sam's car was actually stopping him from worrying too much about his inability to drive. There were a couple of hairy moments along the route, but other than that, everything ran smoothly.

He followed Sam Royston all the way to the factory, which was an odd place for him to come on a Saturday morning but Jackson didn't think too much of it. It was his business after all. Perhaps he had some more work to be getting on with. Jackson pulled up and waited on the side street, keeping an eye on him from a distance and watching as he opened up and went inside. He was only in there for a maximum of five minutes before he was coming out again with a piece of paper in his hand. He studied it, then got back into his car and was soon coming out of the factory car park and heading off on his way, with Jackson in close pursuit. This time, the journey was longer. It was a good hour and a half, and by the time they got there, wherever there was, it was heading on for lunchtime and Jackson was beginning to wish he'd brought some food with him.

So far, nothing particularly exciting had happened, and he was starting to think that maybe Peyton was right. He just hoped his business partner was having some more luck trailing Timmy Rivers.

CHAPTER 25

PEYTON WASN'T. Mainly because there was no Timmy Rivers *to* trail. He caught sight of him inside at one point, but all he did was come into the living room and sit down next to his mother to watch television, sipping on a mug of tea and then eating what looked like a bowl of cornflakes. The two of them remained on the sofa for what felt like hours, but was probably only a matter of minutes. Neither of them were dressed and it didn't look like either of them were planning on putting clothes on anytime soon either. They just sat there in their pyjamas and relaxed, whilst Peyton got more and more bored and slightly jealous, wishing he was at home with the wife watching some old film on Sky.

Eventually, he decided he needed to ring Jackson and see what was going on. They hadn't sent each other any reports as of yet and he'd heard nothing from his partner so he had to assume nothing was going on.

A quick phone call confirmed it, although at least Jackson had had something to do, by the sounds of things.

"I didn't know you could drive," Peyton remarked at one point.

"Ah yes...well...we'll talk about that another time," Jackson quickly avoided the conversation and moved on to other topics, telling Peyton all about the journey to the factory and how they had now just arrived at some other place.

"Do you know where abouts you are?" asked Peyton.

"No idea. I could probably look on Google Maps on my phone but I'll do it when I'm not speaking to you..."

"Yes, OK. What's happening now then?"

"Well...he just pulled up outside some house, so I did too...I'm a couple of cars behind. He's just got out and he's walking towards the door..."

Jackson gave Peyton a live running commentary of what he was seeing as Sam Royston approached the door and knocked. He was still holding the piece of paper in his hand but he now folded it and put it in his pocket as someone answered it.

She was a young woman in her early twenties, and at the sight of Sam she seemed to visibly recoil, taking two steps backwards into her own house again and attempting to shut the door. Sam immediately wedged his foot in at the bottom and curled his two hands round the corner, using all his weight to force it open and push his way inside, slamming it closed again behind him.

The utterly shocked Jackson had, by this point, stopped speaking to Peyton altogether, his mouth ajar in surprise and horror at what he had just witnessed, gazing at the now closed door in amazement.

"Chadwick?" Peyton was saying on the other end of the line. "Are you still there? What's happening now? Chadwick?"

"Er....er yeah, I'm still here," he muttered quietly, then shook his head and cleared his throat, trying to get with it again. "Er...is anything happening where you are because...I think you need to get down here...if you can..." He didn't know what to do. What he had just seen had left an uneasy

186

impression on his mind. The girl had looked terrified and Sam had just barged his way into her house. Why? And what was he going to do now he was in there?

"Why?" asked Peyton, a note of excitement in his voice. "What happened? What did you see?"

Jackson quietly filled him in.

For a while, there was silence on the phone, then he heard the sound of Peyton swallowing. "OK um...can you look at your map and get me the address then?"

"Er yeah...I'll uh...I'll have to hang up."

"Good, fine. Just text it to me."

"Will do."

He hung up. He opened up Google Maps and found his current location. He texted it to Peyton. He did everything in a sort of daze, his mind still replaying what he had seen less than a minute earlier and wondering what the hell he should do next. How long would it take Peyton to get there? Was he round the corner or a long way away? He didn't even know. He was terrible with directions, almost as bad as Peyton was.

Amazingly, he didn't have to wait very long for something else to happen.

The door burst open and Sam Royston emerged, striding back to his car. The girl stood on the step and waved to him, even smiling, although Jackson could read her facial expression even from that distance and could tell the smile was nothing near genuine, and that the gesture was one born out of fear or discomfort rather than an actual desire to bid him goodbye. He had no idea what kind of hold Sam had over this poor woman, but it didn't look good from where he was sat.

Jackson picked up his phone and fired off a quick text to Peyton - 'he's moving again, going to stay with him' - then he waited until he heard the sound of Sam's engine starting up and turned the ignition in his own car merely seconds later, hoping Sam didn't notice the extra sound or the person sat in the vehicle a metre or so away from him with keen eyes watching his every move. Sam was apparently far too caught up in what he was doing as he pulled away from the kerb and set off. Jackson stayed as close as he could and followed him back towards the main road again, picking up his phone to send Peyton continual updates via text message; recklessly taking his eyes off the road to type with one hand whilst keeping one hand on the steering wheel.

'Stop texting me whilst driving!' Peyton eventually replied to one of them, followed by, 'Just message me when you get there. I'm on my way.'

But Jackson didn't know how much longer Sam would keep on driving for, and he didn't want Peyton to get so far behind that he lost them altogether. He continued to send the messages, just quick ones giving the name of whatever street or road they turned into next, slowing down when possible and slightly pulling up into the side to make it safer. He had to make it look like he was keeping his distance anyway so it worked out pretty well, besides which, Sam was continually keeping within the speed limit or less. He seemed to be a fairly safe driver and as such, Jackson ended up being too.

The entire thing was totally exhilarating to him in the meantime; he felt like a proper detective or some kind of super sleuth spy, his brain barely touching upon the possible danger of the situation and trying not to think too hard about what he had seen at the previous house and about what Sam Royston was up to.

CHAPTER 26

Peyton, MEANWHILE, was not driving safely at all, paying little attention to traffic lights or street signs as he whizzed in and out of the other cars on the thankfully relatively quiet roads he was navigating, consistently over the speed limit and keeping his eye out for police as well as everything else. The last thing he wanted was to get pulled now, although he was sure Arthur would be able to get him out of it.

Arthur.

That gave him an idea. He picked up the phone from his lap where it had been resting so he could check his continual updates from Jackson and dialled through to Arthur, turning it onto speakerphone so he could keep driving, then resting it back on his lap again and speaking loudly over the engine noise.

"Arty, could you do me a background check on Sam Royston. Let me know if he's got any convictions or a previous record for anything."

"Sam Royston?" Arthur said in surprise. "I thought you were trailing that Timmy Rivers."

"Timmy Rivers is doing nothing today," sighed Peyton. "It's just an ordinary lazy Saturday. Sam, on the other hand, has just been spotted by my partner doing something...well....for want of a better word...suspicious. That, combined with the argument we heard the other day is....I don't know....there's something going on here, Arty. I don't like to admit it, but there is..."

There was a small pause as Arthur took the information on board, then, "Where are you now?" He asked. "Sounds like you're driving."

"I am," said Peyton. "Jackson's following Sam and I'm following Jackson, or at least, I'm trying to catch up with him. He keeps texting me every time they turn onto a new road but I think I'm a good ten minutes behind him."

"Wait...you're both in different cars?"

"Yeah."

"Well then, Peyt, you're missing an opportunity. If your partner is trailing Sam then that's that angle covered, isn't it?"

"What d'you mean?" Peyton asked, a little confused but willing to take advice off his big brother cop.

"Sam's out. He's not at home, his house is empty. Go and search it. If you think he's up to something suspicious, chances are there'll be at least some evidence of it in his own home."

"But...his wife'll be there..." Peyton protested. "And I don't have a search warrant."

"His record's coming up with an arrest for sexual assault nineteen years ago," Arthur said quickly and seriously. "Charges were later dropped and nothing ever happened with it, but it's enough to get me a search warrant considering what you say your partner just saw."

"Sexual assault? Sam? No way," Peyton almost crashed the car, narrowly swerving to avoid a car that had just stopped at a traffic light and managing to manoeuvre his vehicle into the next lane along. "Are you serious?"

"Yeah, I'm afraid so. It was the first I'd heard about it too."

"Damn, he kept that one quiet. It must have been ongoing whilst I was still working there."

"Yeah, it all happened out of town which was why I never knew about it," explained Arthur. "Merseyside Police have got the full details. Besides which, I never actually looked up his record before. Never thought I would need to either. Still though, this doesn't mean he's done anything. It was just an allegation, that's all."

No more messages had come through during the entire time Peyton had been on the phone to Arthur, but he had to assume that Jackson would be OK. He seemed to be doing fairly fine at taking care of himself and besides which, Arthur was right. He had a good opportunity to go round to Sam's house whilst he was out.

"You think Jackson will be OK on his own?" He asked, speaking his thoughts aloud.

"Course he will, course he will," Arthur reassured him in an almost dismissive tone. "Nothing's going to happen. Just tell him to follow and keep his distance, and keep sending us reports. If anything dangerous happens, call the police straight away and get them down there."

"Us?" Peyton couldn't help but notice Arthur's use of the word.

"Yeah, you can count me on board with this now, Peyt," his brother said. "And just for the record, you're not a bad detective."

The compliment made Peyton's chest swell with pride. He knew those words wouldn't have come easy from his brother's lips considering how much he had doubted him when they'd first started out, but he had little time to dwell on the sensation in the heat of the moment and with everything else that was going on.

"I've got Sam Royston's home address," Arthur continued a split second later, not giving Peyton enough time to respond anyway, and guessing that he was probably too shocked to speak for the time being. "Have you got something to write it down with?"

"I'll remember it," he insisted, doing his best to commit it to memory as Arthur gave him the details. "What now?" He asked.

"I'll meet you there in fifteen minutes with the search warrant and we'll have a look round together. In the meantime, I've placed a call with Merseyside Police to get some more details on this allegation. And get in touch with your partner. Tell him not to take any action. Observe from a distance and if there's an emergency happening, call the police directly."

"Right," Peyton agreed, then, "Arthur?" He asked, a little cautious and unsure. He didn't want to say the words aloud, but the thought was already starting to play around in his mind.

"Yeah?"

"You don't...you don't think Sam could have had anything to do with Gordon's murder do you?"

He heard a distinct sigh from his brother on the other end of the phone. "Gordon Tate committed suicide, Peyton. You're barking up the wrong tree with this murder thing. Whatever Sam Royston's up to, whatever he's involved with and whatever he's threatening Timmy Rivers and this random girl over, it's something completely different, unrelated."

"OK..." mumbled Peyton, trying to take some reassurance from that, although the fact of the matter was, even if it were true, the two of them were still about to get a search warrant and enter the home of a man he had loved and trusted as if he

192

was his own father at one point, and Sam Royston obviously had a few skeletons in his closet regardless.

CHAPTER 27

JACKSON HAD BEEN keeping up with his texts as best he could, but when Sam suddenly pulled up his car and jumped out approaching the door of a residential house on a quiet street, he was transfixed in watching him intently, and had no thoughts of texting Peyton for the time being. He didn't want to miss anything important. This time, however, Sam didn't knock on the door or ring the bell and wait for an answer. He lifted up a garden gnome, reached down and produced a key, which he then used to unlock the front door.

He had a key. Or at least, he knew where it was. Was he breaking in? Or did he own the house?

A dozen questions swam through Jackson's head as he slowly picked up the phone and then gradually turned his eyes away from the now closed front door as Sam disappeared inside and he was left on his own outside in the car. He intended to text Peyton his new location and let him know what he had just seen - that Sam had a key and had gone inside - but then he realised that he'd already received a message from Peyton.

'No longer following you,' it said. 'Gone to Sam's house with search warrant and Arthur. Sam has previous arrest and allegation of sexual assault, no charges. Arty interested enough to want to know more. Stay where you are, keep on him, don't do anything. If something dangerous or illegal starts happening, call me immediately. Kimble.'

Jackson read the message a second time, then frowned and sighed, moving his fingers to respond and letting Peyton know that he understood the request and telling him where he was currently situated. As he did so, his mind was beginning to turn things over and he was getting himself into a bit of a state. He had watched Sam Royston apparently force his way into that girl's house and he had frozen on the spot, unsure of what to do next. He didn't want to panic at the last minute, he wanted to be able to step up to the mark and do the job as he had done on their last case, but this felt different somehow, more important. They were investigating a murder after all.

"Hmm..." He hit the send button on the text and shoved the phone into the pocket of his jeans with another heavy sigh. He looked up and stared at the door of the house for a moment, then leaned forwards and peered round the rest of the street. Seemed like a decent enough area.

He wasn't sure how long they'd been there, but when he looked over to the house again, it was just in time to see the surprising and terrifying sight of Sam Royston emerging from the door with a gun in his hand and approaching Jackson's car, pointing it directly at him.

"Get out," he snapped an order. "Get out of the car."

Jackson gawped at him, unmoving. Where the hell did he get a gun from? Does he just casually keep one in the house? What kind of man were they dealing with here?

"You've been following me all day and I'm not having it, get out of the car. You must think I'm some kind of idiot."

Jackson felt he had no choice but to obey. Sam was already yanking open the driver's side door and he wasn't about to test

196

out his rudimentary judo skills on the gun that was soon being pressed into his temple.

"No fuss now," his captor warned. "You're just going to get out and walk into the house."

CHAPTER 28

PEYTON RECEIVED the message back, and was relieved to know his partner was doing just fine. All he had to do was sit in the car and watch and wait. He doubted very much that there'd be any problems. He, meanwhile, was well on the way to Sam Royston's house, having programmed the address into the Sat Nav and discovered he was only about ten minutes drive away; twelve to be precise.

When he arrived, he only had to wait for a couple of minutes before the recognisable pale blue Mercedes of his brother pulled up a few spaces ahead of him. They clocked each other and gave a sort of nodded greeting as they both got out of their respective cars and walked towards one another.

Arthur took out a piece of paper from his pocket and unravelled it. The warrant.

"Now, let's see if we can find out what's going on with him and Timmy Rivers, and why he went round to that girl's house today."

Peyton gave a single nod of agreement, bracing himself for this latest development in his detecting career. His first official search of premises.

They approached the door and knocked, with Arthur taking the lead in explaining to Sam's slightly confused wife that they had a search warrant for the premises and were coming inside to take a look.

"What is it that you're actually searching for?" She asked them as she reluctantly stepped aside and allowed them access.

"We can't actually tell you that, I'm afraid," answered Arthur apologetically.

Because we don't actually know, Peyton thought to himself, wondering how Arty had managed to swing it to get the warrant in the first place, which strings he had to pull, whose back he had to rub. It was certainly handy having a brother in the police though; it was a wonder he hadn't exploited it at some point in the past.

'We're inside the house,' he sent a quick text to Jackson, keeping him informed of their progress.

"Does your husband have an office at home, Mrs Royston?" asked Arthur. "Somewhere he does business out of hours?"

"It's through the back," she pointed them in the right direction half-heartedly. "First door on the left. But he won't be happy you going in there."

"This will only take a moment or two, Mrs Royston," Arthur assured her patiently. "Then we'll be out of your hair and leave you to your day."

Peyton was impressed. He could tell Arty had done this one or two times in the past at least. The words just tripped off his tongue. He made sure to take it all on board; learning the language so he could say it himself next time, then he followed his brother through to the office.

"This is a good place to start," said Arthur, walking over to the desk and opening up the top drawer. "From what she was saying, I'm guessing his wife doesn't come in here so there's a good chance he'll keep things in here he might not want her to see."

Peyton stood in the doorway for a moment, unsure of what to do next, then he made a move towards the desk. Heading straight for the computer he twirled the screen round to face him, crouched down and rested the keyboard on his knees. "I'll have a look on here."

"Good idea," said Arthur, the two men lapsing into silence.

Arthur scanned through various documents, letters, an address book, everything he could find in the drawers. "What was the address that your partner gave you earlier?" He asked, stopping on one of the pages of the address book.

Peyton took out his phone and scrolled back through the messages, reading out the street name.

"It's in here," said Arthur, spinning his hand round to show Peyton the relevant entry.

"So he knows her then?"

"Would seem that way, yeah. She's not just a random girl. He knows her and he went round there for a reason. Her name's Sarah Brighton."

Peyton stopped what he was doing and frowned. The name seemed familiar to him somehow, but he couldn't place it, he didn't know why.

"What is it?" Arthur asked.

"I don't know...just...I think I know her from somewhere."

"Really? We can do a search for her back at the station, or ring up and get them to do it..."

"Or we can just type her name into Google," Peyton smiled. Still with Sam's keyboard and the monitor set up right in front of him, he was already way ahead of his brother and had done it. "There is more than one way to search for people,

201

y'know...the plebs way." He winked at his brother and hit enter, the smile dropping from his face when he saw the results that came up. He navigated to her Facebook page, saw her picture, along with the list of her previous occupations, and it all clicked into place.

"She used to work at the factory. That's how I know her. She was the secretary for about six months, then she left all of a sudden. Sam said she'd left to have a baby."

Arthur wandered round to the other side of the desk and peered over Peyton's shoulder. "No sign of kids on her Facebook page."

"No...but then people don't always put their kids up, do they? And we're not friends with her so we can't see absolutely all of her profile, only the bits she doesn't mind being public."

"Well, we've got her address," said Arthur. "Maybe we should pay her a visit and ask her directly what Sam was doing there earlier; what he said to her and what their connection is. Maybe he's having an affair or something and he doesn't want his wife to find out. It's not out of the ordinary for bosses to have affairs with their secretaries. Kind of a cliché, but it happens."

"Let's just see what else we can find first," said Peyton, on a bit of a roll with his investigating. "Let's have a look at his e-mails."

"Agreed. You do that, I'll carry on with the rest of the desk." And Arthur went back round again to pick up where he'd left off with his search of the drawers.

It was Peyton who found the next important piece of evidence merely a second or two later. When he went to login to Sam's mail client, a pop up box appeared with a drop down list, giving him a choice of two different e-mail accounts he could access - one in the name of Sam Royston, and the other in the name of Ed Norfolk. He gasped and rocked back on his heels.

"Arty...Sam is Edward Norfolk," he murmured. He clicked the Ed Norfolk e-mail address and the password automatically appeared in little stars in the password box below. Sam, like quite a few other people on their home computers, already had the passwords stored for ease of use. He pressed 'Login' and a moment later had discovered a series of e-mails from 'Ed' to Timmy Rivers, offering him the job as assistant window cleaner and then a couple of others confirming their hours and other arrangements.

Peyton spun the computer screen round so that Arthur could see. "What...what does it mean?" He asked. "Do you think Timmy knows that Ed is actually Sam?"

"I think he does," Arthur nodded gravely. "And I think you know he does too... Think about it, Peyton, you were at Timmy's house today. What happened?"

"Nothing."

"Exactly. On the morning he's supposed to be out window cleaning with this Ed Norfolk he's tucked up at home in bed. He knows who it is alright. So the question is, why? Why would these two men concoct such an elaborate lie together, even to the extent of sending e-mails back and forth?"

Peyton thought about it for a moment, but the answer was fairly obvious. "To construct an alibi."

CHAPTER 29

JACKSON WAS SCARED. He was trying his best not to be, but the situation felt more dangerous and unpredictable than their previous case and besides which, he didn't have Peyton to back him up and make him feel confident and brave. He was entirely on his own as Sam nudged the gun into his back and led him through the hallway of the house and into a room at the back, which turned out to be some kind of pantry. He opened up the door and shoved Jackson inside.

"I know you and Kimble have been sniffing around, asking too many questions," he said to him as Jackson quickly spun round to look at his captor. Sam stood in the doorway, blocking Jackson's exit and pointing the gun straight at his chest.

"Where did you even get that thing from?" He couldn't help but blurt out the question. He'd never seen a gun in his life until the run in with their friendly drug dealer a week ago, and now this. Being a private detective was quite clearly a dangerous profession.

"Internet," Sam answered. "But that's not important. I want you to understand there's no hard feelings. You seem like a nice enough young man, and it's really nothing personal..."

"Right," Jackson muttered sarcastically, trying to give some show of bravado despite at that point being quite worried that Sam was about to shoot him. Why else would he have forced him to come into an apparently empty house and push him into a pantry? And why else would he be saying all these words, that sounded so final, almost apologetic for what he was about to do? He felt his legs trembling slightly. He took a few small steps backwards, holding his arms up in a sort of surrender pose, his eyes looking at him pleadingly. His back hit the wall of the narrow room and he had nowhere else to go.

"I just can't afford to have anyone sniffing around," Sam was saying. "...I've worked too hard for everything to have it taken away from me. I have to cut all ties to the past, make sure everyone stays silent..."

"Everyone? What do you mean?" Jackson asked, seeing a chance to get Sam to open up a bit and besides which, any chance he got to extend the moment before he possibly pulled that trigger was good enough for him. Now, if only he could get to his phone and possibly ring Peyton without Sam seeing. If he just pressed the call button, that might work. But his hands were in the air. How could he move them down casually without Sam noticing and knowing something was going on?

"Give me your phone," Sam suddenly demanded, completely ignoring Jackson's question and seemingly reading his mind. Well, there goes getting him to open up, and there goes his chance of ringing Peyton, Jackson thought to himself, sighing as he slowly lowered his arms and slipped his hand into his pocket. As soon as he removed it, Sam took one step into the room and snatched it from his fingers before he had the chance to do anything else with it.

"Wouldn't want you to be ringing your little friend Kimble now, would I?" Sam grinned, then stepped back again and, without a further word, slammed the door of the pantry. Jackson heard the lock sliding into place but despite that, he leapt for the door and grabbed the handle, rattling and twisting and turning it.

"Let me out!" He banged with his fist.

"I'm afraid I can't do that, mate," he heard Sam Royston's muffled voice say from the other side of the door. "Like I said, it's nothing personal."

Then a set of footsteps receded down the hallway; then nothing.

"Great," Jackson muttered to himself. At least he hadn't been killed though. He breathed a sigh of relief for that and then turned round to have a look round the small cupboard where he'd been locked.

"Ah!" He nearly jumped half out of his skin, yelping and staggering back a bit. In the opposite corner of the pantry, there was someone else sat there - a woman - tied to a chair with ropes, gagged, and apparently asleep, or knocked out unconscious.

He just stared at her for a moment. He didn't know whether Sam had come in and tied her up whilst he'd been sat outside in the car, or whether he'd been keeping her like that for a while. Either way, he needed to untie her and wake her up. Two of them had a better chance of getting out of there than just one.

The room was only about three metres by one, so it took him a split second to stride to where she was seated and drop down at her feet to start to untie her. He hadn't noticed her before when he'd first been pushed into the pantry; too caught up in his own circumstances and aside from that, not actually expecting to see anyone else in there.

The movement of his hands on the ropes and the loosening off of her ties began to rouse her from what must have been an

207

uncomfortable sleep, and she groaned against the gag and fluttered open her eyes, first looking round in confusion and then in fear, immediately starting to struggle and lash about, resulting in Jackson getting a kick to the knee with one of the newly freed feet.

"It's alright, it's alright," he tried to tell her, shuffling back on his heels a bit. "Sam locked me in here too...I'm your friend, OK? I'm here to help. Did Sam lock you in here?"

She nodded and made muffled noises against the gag.

"OK well, I'm sure between the two of us we can manage to break open the door and get out," he tried to give her a reassuring smile then stood up and reached around to take off the cloth that was tied around her mouth. She instantly spat another cloth out onto her lap and swore loudly.

"That slimy creep...I wouldn't do what he wanted so he bloody tied me up...in my own house..."

"What did he want?" Jackson asked, beginning to carry on with the task of untying her fully.

"My silence. I told him to go to hell. Said if anyone came asking, I'd tell 'em the truth. I haven't seen him for years and now he shows up on my doorstep like this...expecting me to just play along, making threats. He didn't even bloody knock!" She continued to rant. "Just let himself in! The cheek of it! After what he did!"

For the most part, Jackson had literally no idea what she was talking about, but he was eager to find out. Right now though, he needed to get her to calm down, so he could hear what she had to say from the beginning. He tossed the ropes to one side and offered out his hand for an introduction.

"My name's Jackson," he said. "Why don't we start with names?"

208

"I'm Tracey," the girl answered, rubbing her wrists from where they'd been made sore from the ropes, then taking Jackson's hand and shaking it.

"How do you know Sam?" He asked.

She sighed and rubbed her eyes. "I used to work for him...at the factory, years ago. I was only temporary cover whilst someone was sick but...well...he...he... raped me..."

Jackson swallowed heavily, his eyes widening. He didn't know Sam very well at all, but Peyton was always saying what a nice guy he was, the revelation came as a bit of a shock, even to him.

"What...what happened?"

"Oh, it was on some work night out or other," she mumbled, looking down, embarrassed. "I got drunk. I barely even remember what happened."

"He might have spiked your drink."

"I think he did," she nodded in agreement, looking back up at Jackson and seeming to grow in confidence as she spoke with him. "Because there's no way I would have agreed to what happened. I remember asking him to get off me at one point, but in the morning, when I woke up in bed, it was all hazy. I spoke to him later on that day and he told me that I'd been well up for it, that I'd wanted it."

"What did you do? Did you press charges? Tell the police?"

She shook her head silently, then carried on. "I was confused. I didn't know what had happened, but the more I thought about it, the more I felt that it was wrong, that I hadn't consented to it. About two days later I got up the courage to confront him and told him I thought he'd raped me, that he'd spiked my drink and then he'd raped me, and that even if he hadn't spiked it, I still hadn't wanted it, I'd still said no and he'd carried on anyway, so it had still been rape."

"Yeah, of course," Jackson agreed sympathetically. "So...so what did you do?"

"He told me that I was an idiot, that this was just me not wanting to admit I'd wanted to sleep with him and that I fancied him. I said that I didn't, and that I was going to report him to the police. He just laughed and said that no one would believe me, but when he saw that I was serious and he started to think that I was really going to go ahead with it, his mannerisms changed. He became aggressive and nasty. He got physical with me...pushed me up against the wall and said that if I ever told anyone he'd kill me. I was...really scared..." At that point, Tracey's eyes filled with tears at the recollection of the terrible events that had happened to her. Jackson grimaced and tentatively reached out a hand to put on her shoulder. He always felt completely self-conscious when people were upset. He didn't know what to say or do or how to comfort them for the best.

"You're OK," he mumbled awkwardly. "Carry on..." He knew it was important that he heard all this, so he could pass the details onto Peyton afterwards, if they ever got out of this mess, although even then, he realised she would probably have to repeat everything again to the official police and again at Sam Royston's trial if it ever got that far. He really hoped it did. To all intents and purposes, the guy seemed like a right bastard who'd got away with it for far too long and had managed to fool the majority of people into thinking he was a decent bloke who wouldn't harm a fly.

"But then," she continued slowly. "After the aggression...he completely changed again...became this completely nice, charming guy again, the guy I recognised from when he first gave me the job, except he had this like....threatening undertone, like we both knew he could do bad things if he wanted. And that was when he offered me money. It was a lot of money. I mean, we're not talking millions obviously because the guy only ran a car business not bloody Microsoft or something, but it was a decent amount...fifty thousand. It was more than I normally earned in a year, and I knew it would pay off all my debts and help me put a deposit down on a house so I could get a mortgage and finally get on the property ladder and stop renting. It was like being given a leg up in life."

"This place," Jackson said. He'd seen the way she'd glanced round the small pantry they were both sat in when she'd mentioned the deposit, and guessed the rest. "You took the money."

"I did," Tracey admitted, a look of shame on her face. "I always felt foolish for it afterwards, because I felt like he'd got away with it, like he'd just bought my silence..."

"Because he had."

"I know...I know...but I kept telling myself it was a good thing, convincing myself it had been the right choice and then eventually forcing myself to stop thinking about it altogether and to try and move on with my life. But it was difficult. It affected all my relationships...I couldn't keep anyone, and even the house itself made me feel strange, reminded me of it, because I knew that his money had helped to secure it. He was always there, at the back of my mind, and what he'd done, and I began to regret not reporting him. I knew it was too late by that point though. Like I said, it's been years...over ten now...and there's no evidence left anymore; just my word against his, and he's a respectable factory owner who everyone loves."

"Not everyone," said Jackson darkly, his eyes clouding over as he thought back to earlier that day and the first house that he had trailed Sam to; the way the girl had looked when she'd opened the door and saw him standing there, the terrified expression, the way he'd grabbed her and pushed his way inside and the way she seemed changed as she stood on the doorstep and gave him a seemingly friendly wave goodbye - changed but still scared. It hadn't been affection that had instigated her wave but fear, and now, in the light of everything he had heard from Tracey, he was beginning to wonder whether there was more than one victim of Sam's savagery.

"Do you know if he's done this to anyone else?" He asked. "I think he might have, but I'm not certain."

"I couldn't tell you, to be honest," Tracey answered. "As you can imagine, I wanted nothing more to do with him after I took his money, even though his face and his words and his actions were never far from my mind. And the last thing I wanted to see this afternoon was his face barging into my house."

"He took the key from underneath the gnome and let himself in," said Jackson, then added as a quick explanation, "I'm a private detective, I've been trailing him all day - saw him do it."

"It doesn't surprise me," she sighed. "He's a sly bugger. Probably hasn't changed a bit since I knew him. I guess he must have watched the house in the past then, or at least driven by here a few times...maybe even followed me home or something. Otherwise how would he know that I keep the spare key there? I've always kept it there; it's a safe area and

212

nothing's ever happened, and I nearly always forget my keys and leave them at work. Then I open up with the spare and the next day lock up with the spare and hide them again. Then try to remember to bring the proper one's home." She managed a smile. Jackson joined in.

"Yeah, I'm terrible with that kind of thing too," he admitted. "What did he say to you today when he turned up at the house?"

"He told me he was just calling round to check up on me, and to make sure I was planning to keep my mouth shut if anyone came sniffing around asking about him. He had that threatening undertone again, and he didn't mess about...he grabbed me straight away and pushed me against the wall, holding me there while he spoke all calm and serious in my ear and pressed that gun of his into my stomach. I suppose he expected me to pee myself and agree to keep quiet immediately, but I didn't. Somehow, even in the face of seeing him again, the guy who had nearly destroyed my entire life, I found this....nerve...this bottle. And I just sort of...laughed...and I told him he could get lost, and that anyone who came asking after him would get the full story and that I'd always regretted not reporting him to the police, that I'd give him up first chance I got and that I hoped all his chickens were coming home to roost. Stuff like that. I just sort of...went off on one."

"Good for you," Jackson laughed and nudged her in the leg.

"Well, not really. I ended up in here, didn't I? The last thing I remember was me taunting him, then he raised up his hand with the gun. I guess he must have knocked me out and then tied me up in here. That must be why I've got a splitting headache."

"Probably," said Jackson, then slowly stood back to his full height again, sighing and turning to the door. "Listen, if you help me get us out of here, I promise we'll get Sam Royston in jail for what he did."

"Yeah of course," she agreed, gingerly standing up, still a little shaken. "Why are you after him anyway?" She asked. "Did you say you were a private detective?"

"I am," Jackson nodded. "Well, an assistant to one anyway. It's sort of a - " And he was about to tell her all about it, when something cut his conversation dead. He sniffed the air once, then twice, frowning. "Can you...can you...smell smoke?" He asked quietly, approaching the door and pressing his face to the small gap in the frame. As if in answer to his question, a thin trail of silvery smoke began to snake through the bottom of the door and into their pantry prison.

CHAPTER 30

PEYTON'S NEXT STEP was to look through Sam's personal e-mails on his other account. They were mostly work related and fairly boring, as it was the same e-mail address he used for the factory as he did for the handful and rare amount of personal e-mails he had. He quickly scanned through them, finding the majority irrelevant apart from one he found saved in the Drafts folder of Sam's account. He had prepared the e-mail as if to send it to himself, but then had saved it, perhaps as a rudimentary way of storing information so that he could open something at work that he had written earlier at home without having to actually send it. E-mails were discoverable documents in law, and could be used against you in court if something ever went wrong and you found yourself facing charges. It was best to be careful with them and avoid sending sensitive information, even to yourself, and when Peyton saw what was inside, he could easily see why Sam had chosen to use this particular method, although still reckless and not as secure as he possibly could have made it. The entire thing smacked of desperation, of someone in a hurry, and after everything he'd discovered so far about the man he thought he knew that day, Peyton was automatically suspicious anyway.

"Look at this," he said, calling Arthur over. "List of women's names and addresses. Six of them in total, including that Sarah

Brighton." He read through the list from top to bottom. "I recognise some of them. I think that girl worked at the factory too," he pointed at the second name as he felt Arthur arrive at his shoulder, then moved to the third name, "she definitely did," the fourth, "don't recognise this one," then the fifth, "nor this one..." Then, at the sixth, he stopped dead, his finger poised over the name on the screen. His heart skipped a beat. He frowned, staring at the letters as if they were in some other language, then slowly turned his head and looked upwards at Arthur. His brother was wearing the same baffled and concerned expression.

"Arthur...why has Sam Royston got our mother's name on his list?"

"HELP!" Jackson and his new found friend Tracey pounded on the door, shoulder to shoulder, both now with a renewed desperation to get out as the smoke began to billow through the gaps and fill their little room. He had no idea what kind of state the house was in outside the pantry, but judging from the state of the smoke, he could make a fairly good deduction that the place was on fire.

So Sam *had* intended to kill them. That was what he'd meant by cutting all loose ends, that it was nothing personal, all that rubbish. Tracey had refused to play ball and so he was killing her, unlike the first girl who he had apparently scared into submission once again. But why now? Why all of a sudden? Just after they'd come in to ask about Gordon Tate's death. And what was the conversation with Timmy Rivers all about?

There were so many loose ends and questions left unanswered, but Jackson didn't have time to think about any of that now. He had to think of a way to get them out of there and fast.

"What are we gonna do?" Tracey whined, frightened and now clinging to Jackson's arm.

"I don't know. Are there no windows in this place?"

"There's one," she answered, approaching one of the storage racks of food and pushing a few tins aside to reveal a tiny window. It was about big enough for a cat to crawl through, but definitely not big enough for them. Still, it was a start.

"Open it up, let some air in. We can shout for help through it too...people might hear us on the street."

A tiny latch only on the small window that was about big enough for a rat to squeeze through and fairly useless to the point where Jackson wondered why someone would build such a stupid window in the first place. In the end, he picked up a tin of beans and smashed out the glass to create a bigger space to let air in, then he scrambled up onto a box so he could reach it better and began to yell through it, just hoping someone was passing by and might hear them.

"HELP! CAN ANYONE HEAR US? HELP!"

CHAPTER 31

NEITHER PEYTON not Arthur knew what the list of six names and addresses meant or what they were for, but the fact that one of them was a girl whose place he had already been round to that day and apparently threatened didn't particularly bode well, and there was something oddly familiar about the fourth address on the list too.

Peyton sent the stored e-mail to print so they could take a copy with them and Arthur went back to his previous search, now moving onto the drinks cabinet stashed against the wall and looking through the two drawers on that.

"Anything interesting?" He asked, twiddling his thumbs a bit whilst he waited for the excruciatingly slow printer to finish its work.

"This..." said Arthur, producing a bottle of pills from the drawer and holding out his arm towards his brother. Peyton took the bottle and looked at the label. It was the same bottle as the one that was found in Gordon Tate's bedroom and it was empty. "I know what you're thinking, Peyt, but like I said before, these pills are fairly common, anyone can get hold of them."

"But these are empty, Arty...why would he keep hold of an empty bottle?"

"Why would he keep hold of an empty bottle if he'd done it? If it implicated him in the crime? Anyway, I thought you didn't want him to have done it?"

"I don't, but everything I'm learning here is making me more and more concerned," said Peyton. "What about the alibi, huh? The window cleaning? Why would the two of them set that up?"

"I don't know. I don't know any more than you do."

"But you can theorise, Arthur. You're a detective...Alan Morrissey was a family friend of Timmy Rivers' parents, so Timmy knew that he was a window cleaner. It would have been easy to find out when his rounds were and where he went. Then all they had to do was concoct this story about Timmy getting a job as an apprentice window cleaner, so that he could approach Morrissey and buy a ladder off him. He got Morrissey to bring him the ladder at work instead of at home, because he didn't want his mum to drop him in it with Morrissey that he hadn't in fact got a job with a window cleaner. Then gone round to Gordon Tate's house at night, after the day Morrissey had done his rounds, so that there'd already be ladder imprints on the ground and no one would get suspicious, put the ladder up against the wall and to go in and murder him."

"Who? Sam Royston?"

"I don't know. But Timmy is involved too. That would explain why they were arguing."

"It's a good theory, Peyton, it really is...but why? What's the motive? And how does it connect to these women on that list, like our own bloody mother?"

"I've no idea," Peyton sighed finding the entire thing completely confusing to the point where it was giving him a headache, but he had been reminded by Arthur of the list, so
220

he walked back to the printer, taking out his phone from his pocket at the same time so he could check for the latest messages from Jackson.

There had been no further updates, but as he glanced through their most recent texts, he suddenly understood why the fourth address had been familiar to him.

"Arty," he snatched the newly printed list from the printer and ran over to his brother to show him. "This one...this address here...that's where Jackson is right now, look," and he showed him the text on his phone to compare. "That's where he trailed Sam to after the first girl, Sarah Brighton."

"He's going through all the women on the list, it would appear," Arthur frowned.

"But not in order. He went to the first address first, and now the fourth address."

Arthur took the list from his hand and studied it. "It's to do with location," he announced. He'd always been much better with directions than Peyton was, and knew the streets of Chester as well as a cab driver might. "The fourth address is fairly close to the first address."

"So...does that mean we can work out where he's going next?" asked Peyton tentatively. "Which address is close to the fourth address?"

Arthur fell silent for a moment whilst he studied them all, then looked up with a grave expression. "Mum's."

Peyton bit his lip.

"But...she's dead."

"Maybe Sam doesn't know that," Arthur theorised.

Peyton frowned. He had no idea what all of this meant, but he knew they had to get to their mum's old house and make sure whoever was currently living there was alright, and

221

preferably arrive there before Sam Royston so they could apprehend him and question him about what he'd been up to; why he'd been visiting these women, threatening at least one of them, and what his involvement was with Timmy Rivers and the death of Gordon Tate.

Peyton looked at his phone again, wondering why Jackson hadn't messaged him. He needed to get hold of him anyway and let him know where they were going, and to find out whether there'd been any sign of Sam leaving yet.

He brought up the recent calls list and then pressed the phone to his ear. It went straight through to voicemail. He frowned and tried again. Still nothing.

"How far is it to the second house, Arty?" He asked, then looked at the list for reference. "Er...Tracey Cartwright's house?"

"About ten minutes, why?"

"It's Jackson. He's not answering his phone."

"Could be out of range. I'm sure he'll call you back," Arthur shrugged.

"Can we just pass by there on our way round to Mum's? I dunno...I just...well, I'm a bit worried. And we need to tell him where we're going anyway. If he's still there then that means Sam is still there."

"That's a good point. Might save us a trip if we go there first."

And so it was agreed. Thanking Sam Royston's wife for her patience, they said a quick goodbye and headed out to their respective cars, deciding between them to take Arthur's. Although it wasn't his official police vehicle, he still had a flashing siren he could stick on the dashboard that blared out and ensured they could skip through traffic lights, drive over

222

the speed limit and have the traffic parted for them along route. As such, a ten minute journey only took them around five. Peyton, sat in the passenger seat, tried calling Jackson a couple more times without success.

As they got nearer and nearer, they noticed smoke in the air, high above the houses, and the sound of more sirens in the distance, getting closer. Someone had obviously called the fire brigade, there was a fire going on.

It was only when they whizzed round the corner onto Tracey Cartwright's road, that they realised it was coming from that actual street, and more specifically, from Tracey Cartwright's house.

Peyton recognised his sister's car parked up on the kerb. That must have been how Jackson got here; he knew he didn't have his own car. The little shit. Still, he had to admire his nerve, and right now he was more concerned about the fire.

Arthur jerked the car to a halt and they both jumped out, running over to Jackson's car to ask him what was going on. It was empty, the door half open, the vehicle abandoned.

"Where is he?" Peyton asked, flustered. The fire in the house looked like it was getting out of control. The glass in the bottom windows had all shattered, with most of them lying on the ground below in blackened shards, the flames entirely engulfed the front living room, and were beginning to lick around the edges of the rooms above as well, black smoke everywhere and quickly spreading.

"I don't know," mumbled Arthur. "Jackson!"

"Jackson!" Peyton joined in the shouting, running over to the house.

"Peyton, keep back!" Arthur warned.

But that was when he heard it. A third voice, shouting, not just their own. A third voice, responding to their calls.

"Help!....help!" It sounded quite faint and distant over the noise of the roaring fire and the crackling and popping of the damaged furniture inside.

Peyton raised his hand for silence and Arthur stopped shouting, the two of them listening some more.

"Help!"

They heard it again, a voice. And it sounded like Jackson's.

Without even thinking twice, Peyton raced into the house and dived through the flames, ducking his head down and holding his arms up around his head, Arthur yelling in vain for him to come back.

Inside the burning heat of the fire, he shouted for Jackson again, listening as he appeared to be getting closer to the calls for help.

"Jackson? Chadwick?"

"Kimble!" He heard his own voice being called in a relieved response, followed immediately by banging, the sounds of fists banging on a door. "Kimble, in here! In here, in the pantry!"

The flames crackled once more and a half burnt painting fell down off the wall and hit Peyton on the shoulder. "Ah!" He grimaced and ducked, getting a mouthful of smoke at the same times. It was getting to his lungs now and the house was falling to bits, he couldn't risk staying in there much longer.

He raced towards the small door on the left hand side near what appeared to be the kitchen at the back, and from where the banging and shouts were coming from. There was a key in the lock. He swiftly turned it and the door flung open from the weight of the two people who had been banging and barging and trying with all their might to get it open - Jackson, and a girl

224

Peyton recognised as being Tracey Cartwright. He had met her once, at the factory. She was a nice woman, pleasant, pretty, easy to talk to.

The pair of them had stripped off the top layers of their clothing to wrap around their noses and mouths, protecting themselves as best they could from the smoke, but they were still weak and spluttering, and looked half dead from exhaustion as they both stumbled out.

"Come on," shouted Peyton, reaching to drag them both up from the floor. "We've gotta get out of here." But as he turned to go back the way he'd come, he realised the fire had spread even further and their pathway was now completely blocked by flames.

The three of them stood for a moment, just staring and paralysed by the fear of the situation, not knowing what to do. It was Tracey who had the first bright idea.

"The back door!" She raised her voice over the cacophony of the fire and tugged them towards the smoke filled kitchen. Peyton grabbed a chair and hurled it at the glass door. They didn't have time to look for keys. The glass shattered and sprayed outwards, and the sudden gush of oxygen seemed to increase the roar of the approaching flames even more.

The three of them raced out, their arms raised to their heads and their faces down to protect them from getting cut by the glass, then proceeded to take large, eager gulps of the fresh air, still spluttering even as it filled their lungs.

The glass in the window above them popped, sending shattered shards raining down on them as Peyton quickly ushered the other two round the side and back to the front of the house just as two fire engines and an ambulance were pulling up, and a frantic Arthur gesticulating and telling the emergency services that there were people inside the house.

He looked as relieved as ever Peyton had seen him when he spotted them emerging from round the side, and instantly they were approached by paramedics who led them over to the back of the ambulance to make sure they were alright.

"I'm fine," Peyton insisted, not wanting to be fussed over. He was a little singed round the edges, but Jackson and Tracey had been in there for longer, and needed more attention. Still though, he had questions, and he wanted answers.

"Where's Sam?" He asked his partner.

"Probably long gone," Jackson shrugged. "He locked us in there, set the place on fire and left us to burn."

Peyton and Arthur looked at one another, the shock that Peyton was feeling at realising the man he had once respected held so many dark secrets close to his chest was now far outweighed by the immediate fear he felt for a whole new bunch of people. A family had moved into their old house after their mother had died and she was next on the list. He didn't know the full story as to why Sam had locked them in and set the place on fire, but he could hear that later. He didn't want to stick around here if someone else was at risk.

"I'm sorry, Jackson, but we have to go," he said apologetically, using his first name. Now was no time for playing at detectives and formalities. "Our mother's on his list and we think he's going there next. Will you be alright here?" He was already beginning to stride away with Arthur.

"What? Wait a second!" Jackson shrugged off the red blanket that the paramedics had draped over his shoulders and ran to catch up with Peyton. "Nan's dead, I don't understand. What list?"

226

"We found a list in Sam's house," Peyton began, then quickly filled him in on the details, including the two e-mail accounts, and the empty bottle of pills.

Jackson gulped and bit his lip, then glanced back between Tracey and Peyton. "There's...there's something I have to tell you too. I think...I think that list is a list of women Sam Royston has raped."

"Raped?" Peyton immediately thought back to the sexual assault allegation that Arthur told him about, the one that had been dropped years ago. Could he have done more things like that?

"What makes you think that?" He asked.

"Tracey," said Jackson. "She was one of his victims. Listen, just take me in the car with you, I'll explain everything on the way, alright?"

Peyton thought about it for a second, then quickly nodded in agreement and the three of them dashed to Arthur's car.

CHAPTER 32

By THE TIME they arrived at their old family home, they were too late. After knocking on the door and speaking to the man who lived there with his wife and two kids, they confirmed that someone matching Sam's description had indeed been there merely five minutes earlier, but had left in a hurry when they explained that Mary Kimble had died some years ago.

The group of three thanked the man and dived back into Arthur's car to make haste to the next nearest location on the list, feeling like this was some kind of race against time to get there before someone else got hurt.

"That's Sam's car!" Jackson pointed, their tyres screeching as Arthur pulled them to a quick stop and they all jumped out, running towards the already open front door of the house. They could hear shouting and raised voices from inside and the three of them burst through into the living room to see Sam Royston manhandling a frightened young woman on the sofa, his strong hands pinning her upper arms down as he towered over her, leering and threatening, snarling into her face.

"You'll do as I damn well say!" was all they got to hear of the confrontation, before Arthur and Peyton both grabbed him - an arm each - and yanked him backwards.

Sam was taken by surprise, but he was still a fairly agile man despite his age, and managed to spring to his feet and quickly turn away from the two of them, but that was when he ran straight into Jackson, who was blocking the door.

Definitely wanting some kind of revenge for getting locked in a burning house, Jackson made a tight fist with his right hand and swung it straight into Sam's stomach with a satisfying thud. The man doubled over, the wind knocked out of him, and that split second of a moment was all the other two needed to gain the upper hand.

Soon, Arthur had snapped on the handcuffs and was leading their new prisoner outside. He didn't need to question him about his involvement immediately; he could arrest him on charges of arson, then get the full story later, but more than anything, Arthur and Peyton wanted to know why their mother's name had been on Sam's list.

When confronted with the evidence Peyton and Arthur had found in his home, and with the statement of Tracey Cartwright, Sam Royston cracked under pressure and admitted everything, at least, almost everything. He confessed that the list of women was a list of his six victims. He had saved it to his e-mail account and then gone into work to print it off that morning before setting out to visit the first victim, initially unaware that Jackson had been following him right from the beginning.

It was a massive blow to both Peyton and Arthur to learn that their mother Mary had been amongst Sam's victims. Even though the crime had taken place over thirty years ago now, it still felt fresh and raw for them, because they had only just discovered it, and the fact that Sam had been getting away with it all this time infuriated them.

"I can't believe I thought I knew that guy," Peyton shook his head as he sat out in the corridor at the police station, Jackson next to him. Arthur had been inside the interrogation room questioning Sam for a good hour or so, but he'd been keeping the pair of them up to date due to the fact that they weren't officially allowed inside because they weren't considered professional detectives by law. Peyton could just tell by Arthur's mannerisms that things would be different now though; that he'd changed his opinion of them and was on their side. He knew they were good detectives, that they could make a career out of this.

"He fooled pretty much everyone though, Kimble," said Jackson supportively. "Not just you. I mean...even his wife. I'm betting she doesn't know that her husband is an occasional serial rapist and a murderer."

"Well, we don't know about the second part yet."

"We soon will do though," Jackson nudged Peyton in the ribs and they both looked towards the door as Timmy Rivers was brought in for questioning, a police officer on either elbow. He looked nervous and edgy. Peyton guessed he'd probably already been told of Sam Royston's arrest, and although he longed to hear the interview, he continued to sit and wait outside as Arthur came out to greet Rivers and lead him to another interrogation room separate from Sam.

"Maybe next time Uncle Arthur will manage to pull some more strings and let us sit in on the questioning," Jackson said hopefully.

"It all depends on whether my theory is correct," mumbled Peyton.

"I like your theory a lot," smiled Jackson. "But your brother was right. It was still lacking a motive. What was Sam's motive for killing Gordon?"

CHAPTER 33

"THE RAPES," Arthur Kimble gruffly announced, straightening out his shoulders as he stood in front of Peyton and Jackson, breaking down the results of his interrogation. "That was the motive missing from your wonderful, and mostly correct, theory."

Peyton's eyes widened more from the fact that his theory had been mostly correct than anything else.

"Gordon Tate found out that Sam had raped someone. You know how his father said he was keen? Well, he stayed behind late one time to do some extra work; came round knocking on Sam's private office, and found him in there having his way with the latest secretary he'd taken on. She was trying to fight him off, he was forcing her down and stripping off her clothes. Sam barked at Gordon to get the hell out, so he did do. Then, when he'd finished the uh...deed, he took Gordon aside and expected him to fall into line, to not tell anyone. After all, Gordon was going to inherit everything if he behaved himself - the entire factory."

"But Gordon didn't play ball," Peyton took over the story, managing to fill in the rest of the gaps himself. "He went off the rails a bit, bought some weed off our favourite local drug dealer, mumbled stuff about going to the police. He couldn't keep such a shameful secret to himself. Gordon was a good kid; never did anything wrong."

"That's right. I doubt he even knew about the other rapes, but just one was enough, and when it became clear to Sam that he couldn't control him anymore, he decided to take drastic action. He chose someone else to take over from him after he retired."

"Timmy Rivers," Jackson guessed.

"That's right," nodded Arthur. "That's how he brought him on board, got him involved in the sick little plan of his and persuaded him to carry out the deed for him, in exchange for the factory. And Timmy, not being half the moral man that young Gordon was, readily agreed. They set up the false alibi, and then it was Timmy who propped the ladder up against Gordon's wall and snuck in to give him the drugs whilst he was sleeping, set up the suicide note and make it look like he'd taken his own life. With the slightly odd way that Gordon had been acting in the past couple of days and the fact that he'd bought weed - something so apparently out of character for him - they were certain they'd get away with it and that no one would suspect it was anything other than a suicide. They weren't banking on two eager detectives such as yourselves..."

At that point, Arthur smiled rather proudly and gave Peyton a hearty clap on the shoulders.

"You've done well, Peyt," he said. "I'm sorry I doubted you...and I'm afraid I have one more little mystery for you to clear up before this is all done and dusted."

"What's that?" Peyton asked, eager as always to take on a new challenge.

"Our mother."

Peyton's eyes darkened at the mention of her. Although they did not yet know the full details, they knew for certain that she was one of Sam Royston's victims, that he had raped her.

"According to Sam, it happened around thirty years ago," said Arthur. "The thing is...the date's coincide with...with..." He trailed off, but he didn't need to finish the rest of the sentence.

"Our brother."

"That's right."

"That's why she gave him away."

"Do you think so?" asked Arthur. "I was certainly considering the idea, but I wanted your opinion on it."

"Well, it makes sense now, doesn't it? That's why Dad was so insistent. And maybe that's why they broke up not long after. Dad couldn't stand it. The secret..."

"But why did she keep it a secret, Peyton? Why not go to the police?"

"Why did any of them keep it a secret? Fear? Bribery? We'll never know."

"Unless we confront Dad."

"We don't even know where he lives anymore," sighed Peyton. "We could look him up, I suppose. Some other time..." He rubbed his eyes. "This case is over. We need to go and tell Ainsley Tate we caught his son's murderer. Give him the full details." He glanced across at Jackson, who was looking quite confused at the mention of their other brother. He would fill him in on the drive over.

"Yes, you do," Arthur agreed, holding out his hand for a shake.

Peyton clasped his brother's hand warmly. "Our brother is out there somewhere, Arty. And this whole thing has only made me more determined to find him, all over again." The old enthusiasm for the hunt was back, and he could see that Arthur was pleased about it too. "And as long as the Kimble Detective Agency is around," he added. "Then it's only a matter of time before he's found."

"Hey, that rhymes," Jackson pointed out excitedly. "Can that be our motto? Or something like that."

"We're not having a motto, Chadwick," grumbled Peyton.

"Aw come on, please, Kimble."

"No."

With the big red phone at their office bursting with voicemails, a brand new case ready to be tackled at Sherri's school, a feature about to get published in the local paper regarding their important and crucial role in the capture of serial rapist and murderer Sam Royston and his accomplice, and the mystery of their 'born of rape' brother still to be solved, the future was just beginning for the Kimble Detective Agency, with the now sealed friendship of Peyton Kimble and Jackson Chadwick, and the assured assistance of elder brother Arthur Kimble, a new adventure was waiting for them right around the corner.

Made in the USA
Charleston, SC
15 November 2014